STICK

Also by Michael Harmon

ST⚡CK

Michael Harmon

Alfred A. Knopf

New York

THIS IS A BORZOI BOOK PUBLISHED BY ALFRED A. KNOPF

Text copyright © 2015 by Michael Harmon
Jacket art copyright © 2015 by Jennifer Heuer

Visit us on the Web! randomhouseteens.com

Educators and librarians, for a variety of teaching tools, visit us at RHTeachersLibrarians.com

Library of Congress Cataloging-in-Publication Data
Harmon, Michael B.
Stick / Michael Harmon.—First edition.
p. cm.
Summary: "Stick, a star football player who's become disenchanted with the game, becomes friends with Preston, a nerdy kid who fights crime by night."
—Provided by publisher
ISBN 978-0-385-75436-1 (trade) — ISBN 978-0-385-75437-8 (lib. bdg.) —
ISBN 978-0-385-75438-5 (ebook)
[1. Interpersonal relations—Fiction. 2. Football—Fiction. 3. Fathers and sons—Fiction. 4. Friendship—Fiction. 5. High schools—Fiction. 6. Schools—Fiction. 7. Spokane (Wash.)—Fiction.] I. Title.
PZ7.H22723Sti 2015
[Fic]—dc23
2014041400

The text of this book is set in 11-point Berling.

Printed in the United States of America
August 2015
10 9 8 7 6 5 4 3 2 1

First Edition

This book is for all the
superheroes out there,
on and off the field.
Thank you for making
the world a better place.

1

I was there. In the zone. Midair, my body stretched, flying right along with the football. I loved the feeling. Those few seconds when nothing was touching me. When I was free. When I was doing what I loved and the rest of the world disappeared. Game winner. Touchdown. Cheering crowd. We would put another notch in the belt, show the league who would dominate. Just like last year. State champions. First time in school history to take it twice in a row. Second time in state history any school had swept two years.

It skimmed my fingers. Fell away. Like a dream you could barely grasp after waking: there, but not there.

I hit the field, thudding and skidding on the turf, the ball tumbling away uselessly. Dream over. Game over. Back to real life.

Driving home, I replayed it in my head a million times.

Our first loss of the year. Me picking myself up. Feeling the bruises forming, the adrenaline leaving my veins. The crowd quiet. Coach with a slack-jawed expression. My dad on the fifty-yard line, four rows up in the stands, manning the video camera. His face wasn't disappointed. No. Not one bit disappointed.

He was sitting in his recliner when I got home. Four empty beer bottles, and a fifth, half full, sat on the table next to him. I shut the door. He hit the pause button on the remote and nodded toward the couch. "Sit down, Brett."

I took a breath, walked across the carpet, and sat. Of course he was replaying the game, and of course it was paused exactly at the spot where I missed the pass. The past three years of my life—since I'd made it onto the Hamilton team at the start of freshman year—had been paused on every mistake I'd ever made on the field. He took a swig of his beer. "Perfect pass, Brett. Perfect."

"I couldn't get to it."

He grunted, then jabbed the remote at the TV like he was poking a fire. He rewound the tape. "No. Watch." He hit the play button, and we watched the down from beginning to end. "See? What do you see?"

My shoulder ached. "Me missing a pass."

He looked at me, never happy with anything but total perfection. His eyes went back to the screen. "Why, though? Why did you miss it?"

My knees were killing me, and the only thing I wanted was to zone out, but no, he had to teach me. Show me everything I wasn't. Show me everything he'd never been. "I'm tired, and I've got to train in the morning. Can we do this tomorrow?"

He nodded, chugging the rest of the beer and getting up. "Yes, we're going to do this tomorrow. But we're also going to do this tonight." He pointed at the screen as he passed to get another beer. "What did you see, Brett?"

"I saw a long pass."

I heard him pop the cap on a fresh one. He walked back in and sat down, tipping the bottle at me. "It can't always be somebody else's fault. You were late on the snap. Look." He hit rewind and played it again. "See? That half second meant you would have been where you should have been. It wasn't a long pass. You should have been there."

My father was an avalanche of ice spilling over me, but instead of stinging and burning, I was just numb. He was relentless. Obsessed.

"It was one pass, Dad."

He finished his beer. Less than three minutes from full to empty. He shook his head. "Exactly. One pass. Losers lose, and you lost because you didn't pay attention."

I grunted, glancing at the beer bottle still clutched in his hand. "You didn't happen to notice the four I caught? Or maybe that I went for ninety-seven yards? Or maybe that my room is full of trophies?"

"Don't start with the bullshit, Brett. I'm tired of your attitude, and on top of that, I know you're failing math, which means no football." He shook his head and tried to take a swig of the bottle, which was empty. He looked at it, irritated, then tipped it at me. "Yeah, Coach called. You're failing. I don't know what your problem is, but we've got a scout from UCLA coming to look at you next week, and I'm not going to let anything ruin that. Including tonight. What if he'd been here? What if he'd seen it?"

You could give my dad a penny less than a million dollars and he'd bitch about the penny. And I knew he really didn't want to know what my problem was. If he knew, he'd flip. "He would have seen me miss a long pass."

He shook his head, his eyes bleary. "You want to be a smart-ass? Fine. Grounded for the weekend. Forced manual labor. Go to bed."

"Dad—come on. So I should have caught the pass. I'll watch the tape tomorrow, and I'll work on the snap."

He shook his head. "Grounded. At least until you buck up." He raised an eyebrow at me. "And lose the attitude, huh? This isn't Little League. You're not playing with a bunch of little pukes with no talent. You're a champion."

Relentless. It never ended. "There's a party tomorrow night. The whole team is going to be there. Please?"

"I said grounded." He held out his hand. "No phone, either. Not until you bring that grade up."

I bit my lip, tempted to stuff the phone down his throat, but I handed it over. He threw it on the table, then went back to watching the screen. I watched him watching me fail, and I knew why I was in trouble. And math had nothing to do with it.

2

Three years of waking up at five in the morning, seven days a week, rain or shine, vacation or not, has a tendency to create a habit. I didn't need an alarm anymore. Every day of my life began the same, and I looked forward to it. Roll out of bed, throw on whatever gym clothes I had lying around, and run five miles along the bluff overlooking the Palouse hills. Then it was back home, eat breakfast, head to the gym, hit the weights for an hour, shower, dress, and go to class. After school I'd hit the gym or the field, depending on the time of year, and train more.

It was grueling, but I loved it. I loved working my body, because I could see a difference. I could run faster, lift more, go longer. The more I worked, the better I got. My dad and my coach couldn't take that away from me, and when I ran those miles and worked those weights, the hollow pit in my stomach that I got from thinking about how much I hated football disappeared. Just like when I hit the field at the beginning of a game.

How I could hate something so much and love it at the same time escaped me. Insanity at its best.

After a weekend doing forced manual labor to pay for the ultimate sin of not catching a ball, I caught up with Mike Jackson, otherwise known as my best friend and teammate. Sixth period was over, and he stood with Jeff Lions and Tilly Peterson, both linebackers, laughing, talking, and joking their usual bullshit. I joined them, slapping five. School was out, and we were free. Hundreds of students hustled through the indoor courtyard, streaming down the stairs, milling around and talking before leaving for the day.

Mike and I had met in detention, of all places, back in sixth grade. He'd mouthed off to his teacher, and I'd been busted for flicking a carrot at Naomi Wilson during lunch. We'd discussed our punishments in whispers, each coming to the conclusion that our crimes had been well worth the punishment. I'd scored a direct hit on Naomi's forehead, and Mike just plain liked mouthing off to teachers.

Since then, we'd been glued at the hip. Sixth-grade summer camp, trips to the mall, hanging at the skate park, walking around downtown looking for hot girls. When I'd tried out for the football team in seventh grade, Mike joined me, and even though he didn't know a touchdown from a field goal, he made it. Big for his age, he was pretty agile, and knew how to hit naturally.

"Yo, Stick," he said, holding his hand out.

I slapped him five. They called me Stick because I had sticky fingers. Good at catching things, which meant everything at this school. "Sorry I missed the party."

"Dude, I tried to call you like five times. It was awesome."
I shrugged.

He knew the story without me having to tell it. "The pass? He really grounded you because you missed the pass?"

I nodded.

Jeff laughed and punched my arm. "Check it. Show's about to start."

"What show?"

He leaned close and pointed across the way. "See Donny Dorko over there?"

I looked, and a kid, a freshman by the looks of him, sat on a bench near the foot of the stairs. Skinny, small, and with blondish hair, he sat with one knee crossed over the other, reading a comic book. He absently bit his fingernail, head down and intent on the magazine. "Yeah, so?"

Tilly, his big face eager, gave me a devious look, then pointed up. Four more guys from the team, one of them Lance Killinger, our infamously egotistical quarterback, stood at the railing of the second floor, looking directly down on the kid. Tilly made eye contact with them, barely nodding. They laughed and gave a thumbs-up. Tilly put two fingers to his lips and let out an ear-splitting whistle. Everybody in the place stopped, the whistle echoing off into nothing. Everybody stared at the huge linebacker.

At the sudden quiet, the kid looked up, his eyes going to Tilly. Then Tilly smiled and pointed a massive arm at the kid. All eyes went from Tilly to the boy, just as the guys upstairs released what they were holding. I watched as four eggs fell, glinting white in the afternoon sun like silent and graceful missiles.

If one thing is true, most athletes are above average when

it comes to hand-eye coordination. All four eggs exploded on the kid's head and shoulders, the cracking noise echoing as the slimy yolks cascaded over him. Tilly slapped his hands together, pumping his fist and bellowing through the courtyard. "Ladies and gentlemen, now that is a DIRECT HIT! FUCKING AWESOME!"

Laughter erupted, and I stood there as it continued. Some people, mostly girls, voiced their disgust, but nobody did anything about it. Of course they didn't. This was school. Nobody ever did anything. I looked at the kid, expecting him to do what he *didn't* do.

He didn't do anything. He sat there, unmoving, egg dripping from him, no expression on his face, his eyes on Tilly. Then he looked down to his comic book, slowly turned the page, and resumed reading.

Jeff laughed. "Awesome."

Tilly was so typical, it was disgusting. I shook my head, hating myself in an instant for being just another person who didn't do anything. Tilly was the joker of the team, but after three years of it, the thin line between fun and just plain mean was blurring. "What did he do to deserve that?"

Tilly crossed his eyes at me. "He was born, dude. That's why. Don't be an idiot."

"Hey, Till? You're an asshole."

He laughed, slapping my shoulder just hard enough to let me know who was running the show. "Jesus, Stick, put your angel wings away, huh? Stop being a bitch."

I looked at him, and suddenly I hated him. I'd never really had much respect for the guy, but now, looking at how much enjoyment he was getting out of what he'd done, I

8

would have loved to see him go head-to-head with a speeding train. I faced him. "I got a question for you, Till. Why do you always do stuff to guys who can't possibly beat the living shit out of you?"

It took a few seconds for him to understand that I'd questioned the basic rule of what being a complete dick was all about.

I nodded when he didn't answer. "You know Darren Sanwick? He was in science with us last year? The guy with five black belts in jiu jitsu? Fights in the cage every month out at the casino? Yeah—him. The guy who could destroy you in less than a minute," I said, staring at him. He still didn't answer. I went on. "Why don't you pull that crap on him?"

Tilly smiled, but there wasn't a smile in his eyes. Our football team, just like any other team, had a pecking order, and I'd just pecked the wrong way. "It's just a joke. Come on."

"Not really, Till. It's not. It just shows you're a pussy. And you're mean," I said, then turned around and walked away. As I did, I glanced at the kid. He stared at us, a completely neutral look still on his face. He had no chin, big dark eyes, and pale skin. Then he slowly closed his comic book, put it neatly in his egg-splattered backpack, got up, and walked out the doors like nothing had happened.

I imagined him walking or taking the bus home, a public example of what happens when you're born to be slowly beaten into nothing more than a warm bag of humiliation. I knew what the kid's life was and what it had always been. One look at him and anybody would know he was the butt of every joke, the target of endless pranks, and I couldn't imagine how he could live with it every day. The eyes on you. The laughter. Always expecting something to happen and knowing you were too weak to do anything about it. A part of me understood why guys like him came to school and put bloody holes in things with high-caliber weapons.

I heard running feet from behind and turned. Mike came up to me. "Hey," I said.

He glanced back at the guys. "Hey. What's up with you and Tilly?"

I pointed out the doors, where the kid had gone. "You're good with that?"

"What? The kid?" he said, shrugging. "Lighten up."

I wondered if Mike was changing into something I didn't know, or if I was the one who was changing. "So, you are good with that?"

"I'm not the bad guy here. I didn't have anything to do with it." He smiled then. "Watching isn't a crime, bro."

"No, it's not. But I don't think it bothers you, and that bothers me."

He smirked. "Since when does anything bother you? You're like a little tin soldier doing exactly what he's told. Can't you ever just have some fun?"

I could have fun. But I wanted to walk up to that kid. Make him somehow feel better. But I didn't. Couldn't. I never did. I just shut my mouth and did what was expected. Mike was right. I was the best high school wide receiver the state of Washington had ever seen, and I needed to protect that. "That's not fun to me."

"Well, you're putting it all on me, and that's not cool."

I thought of my dad. Of Coach Williams. Of math. "I

know you wouldn't do that shit, but when is it all enough? When is it too much?"

He studied me, a question in his eyes. "What are you talking about?"

"Everything. This whole school. The team. Sometimes it seems like it's just all fake. Like a pretend world. Like we're something better than all the dregs. Isn't that what Coach tells us? That we're better than everybody else?"

"Weekend that bad?"

Mike knew about my dad. The real dad. Not the greatest, most cool sports dad to everybody in the outside world. "Let's just say that Coors Light stock isn't going down."

3

The next day, Coach Williams's massive frame darkened the doorway from his office into the gym. His voice bellowed over the screeching tennis shoes and bouncing balls. "Patterson, in my office. Now."

I looked up, midshot, the ball frozen in my hands. I watched him disappear into his office, slamming the door shut. Mike pivoted inside, stole the ball, and landed a crazy weird hook shot. Free period was almost over, and I hadn't even broken a sweat. Not until I heard those words.

Mike laughed. "C'mon, Stick, stay on the ball, man."

Most seniors had a free period, and instead of going to study hall or the library, I shot hoops to get my mind off things. "Crap."

Mike dribbled the ball around me and landed a perfect layup. "Go, man. He'll have you cleaning his toilet with your tongue if you don't."

I walked across the gym, knowing Mike was right. I reached the door and knocked.

"Get in here."

I opened the door. Coach Williams sat behind his desk, hands clasped over his fat belly, Nike visor perched high on his forehead. He'd played three years for the Dolphins back during the Stone Age, coached like an ex–NFL player on crack, and didn't take crap from anybody. He lived and breathed football, and I would have bet a thousand dollars his DNA code was strung together with pigskin. "Hey, Coach."

He pointed to the chair. The chair could be either a good place or an incredibly bad place, and I had a feeling today it would be the latter. I sat looking at him. He picked up a piece of paper, crumpled it, and threw it at my chest. I flinched as it bounced to the floor. Silence.

Coach Williams, besides being the best yeller I had ever known, could intimidate a person even more with the opposite. Utter, stone-cold, piss-your-pants-because-you-know-something-really-very-bad-is-going-to-happen silence.

I looked at him, and his black eyes swallowed me whole. "I can bring my grade up, Coach. I can."

His answer was the muscles of his jaw pulsing as he clenched his teeth.

Resigned, I looked down. "Whatever."

His hand slamming on his desk made me jump as high as the penholder, stapler, coffee mug, and team picture of the Miami Dolphins did. His voice came low and sharp. "Tell me the first rule of football at this school, Brett, and by the way, if you ever say 'Whatever' to me again, I'll run you till you puke your lungs out."

Coach had no tolerance for two things. One was weakness; the other was anybody daring to mouth off to him. I'd seen him cut a first-string running back for calling him an asshat. First-string. Off the team. Done.

Coach pointed to the sheet of grades crumpled on the floor. "We're not talking calculus or physics or honors, Patterson. We're talking math. Plain and simple math. Count-on-your-fingers-and-get-an-answer math. So tell me the first rule of football at this school."

"Grades, sir."

He continued. "You know what happens when you fail math at this school?"

"Yessir."

He crossed his arms over his chest. "Then why don't you tell me, Mr. Brilliance? Tell me what happens."

"It means I don't play football."

He clenched his teeth. "If it were that simple, my life would be a piece of frickin' cake, Patterson. I know you can catch a ball, but why don't you put whatever brain you have to use and tell me what it really means."

I shrugged.

He shook his big head, took his visor off, and threw it on the desk. "You fail math, you don't play. That's the easy part. The bigger part is that you let down your team, you let down your school, you let down your dad, and you let down the game itself. You've got a chance at a full-ride scholarship *this weekend* with the scout from UCLA visiting, and we've got a chance at another state championship at the end of the season." He paused, staring at me. "You going to blow your future because you can't count on your fingers?"

"I'm not stupid. Math is just hard for me. I try."

He blinked, intense and unrelenting. "Is your dad made of money? You got, like, a money tree growing in your backyard? I've known him for twenty-five years, and I've never seen one in your yard. Am I missing something here?"

I met his eyes. "I said I'm not stupid."

He jabbed a finger at me. The same finger he'd jabbed at me since I was a freshman. "You don't tell me what you think you are or aren't, Patterson. You are exactly what I say you are, and nothing else. People pay over a hundred thousand dollars to get an education at UCLA. And they want to *give* it to you for free, and you can't pass caveman math. *That . . . ,*" he said, hitting his desk again, "is *stupid.*"

"I talked to my teacher. He said I could—"

Coach slammed his hand down loudly for the third time. "You know what, Patterson? I don't care what you have to say, and I don't care what your teacher has to say. As long as you're on my field, you don't fail. You got that? And it also means you play by my rules and my rules only. We've worked the snap into eternity, and you were late on it. So make your decision. Right here, right now, make it. You pull your head out of your ass and get your game on, or you walk."

I looked at him and he looked at me, and I knew in an instant he could see right into my soul. He could see the truth. I studied his face. "You're afraid, aren't you, Coach? You're afraid that I'm not afraid of you anymore, huh?"

His face hardened. "Don't go down that road, Brett. You don't want to see where it ends."

Right then I knew what I was to him. I was a pair of hands and a ticket to his glory. That's all that mattered to anybody. Winning, and winning at all costs. This was insane. My dad, the team, Mike, and that football field under the lights flashed through my mind. But it was now. It was here. I was tired of being afraid, and for some reason, the kid with the egg splattered all over him looked up at me and grinned through it all. "Maybe I do want to see where it ends."

He picked up the phone, threatening me. "You want this? You want me to drag your father in here so we can hash it out? See what he says? Because right now, you're one smart-assed word away from sitting the bench for a game."

My heart slowed, and a clarity came over me. It was so simple. I'd spent so much time sweating this, but it was really that simple. "You won't bench me."

His eyes widened for just the slightest moment before his bluster came back.

I saved him a response. "You can't win state without me."

He smiled, an ugly smear crossing his face. "You think I haven't been leveraged before, son?"

I shrugged, my eyes meeting his. "You can't win without me."

He took a moment, the little mice in his head turning his wheels. "This game isn't about one person, Brett. It's about working as a team. It's about trust and dedication and hard work. It's about accomplishing a goal."

I almost laughed. Football was about power and control and fear and intimidation, but more than anything else, it was about winning. And Coach Williams had proved it

16

for years. I'd seen him play injured guys. I'd heard him tell players to target opponents. He'd do anything to win, and he'd use anybody in order to do so. I stood.

"What do you think you're doing?"

"I'm walking down that road." Then I left.

Sixth period dragged on and I got the call to go to the office after class. The wheels had begun to spin, and I knew what I was in for.

I looked at the kid sitting across from me in the office and my stomach crawled. Donny Dorko. Egg-splatter man. The kid I didn't want to think about because he reminded me of what I hadn't done.

I shifted uncomfortably as I waited for my counselor. I knew I could thank Coach Williams for being called in. "Hey."

He said nothing, just sat there. Hunched over a bit, his elbow on his knee and his palm under his chin, he stared at the floor.

I thought of what Mike said. He hadn't had anything to do with it, and I hadn't either. Just happened to be there when it happened. Not a crime. I took a breath. Somehow, that was a lame excuse. I *did* feel like I was a part of it, and I knew why. "I didn't have anything to do with yesterday."

He bit his lip, studied the floor, and then looked up at me without straightening his hunched shoulders. His eyes were big and brown, his skin pale. "Biologically impossible."

I frowned. "Huh?"

His voice was lower than I thought it would be, and tinged with sarcasm. He reminded me of a frog. He went on. "Unless you can suddenly not exist for a period of time, all matter that existed yesterday had something to do with yesterday. Rocks, trees, dirt, people. All matter."

I sat back, slouching my shoulders. Great. Weird on the outside and weirder on the inside. "Whatever."

He kept those eyes on me but said nothing.

I clenched my teeth, frustrated. "I was just saying I didn't have anything to do with yester— With the egg thing."

He turned his head down and stared at the floor again, methodically drumming his fingers against his lips.

I sat, waiting, and he said nothing. I tried again. "It was uncool."

When he finally spoke, his voice was deadpan, completely unemotional, and awkward. He blinked. "Is this some kind of sad and pathetic way to apologize while admitting nothing while at the same time making me think you're saying sorry for something you apparently had nothing to do with?" He looked at me. "Or are you gay and this is your way of hitting on me?"

"No . . . No! Jesus, I was just saying I didn't know anything about it. I didn't know what was happening."

He nodded, then resumed his hunched-over position. "It's fine to be gay, but I'm not a homosexual. Sorry."

I looked at him, and I could tell, for some odd reason, that he wasn't being sarcastic. "I'm not gay, and I am sorry. I should have stopped it."

"Stopped what? The hands of time? The sun from rising? Idiots from being idiots?"

I propped my head back against the chair, closing my eyes. "So, what's your name?"

"Preston Underwood."

"Why're you here?"

"I'm an undercover agent. There's a drug ring here at the school. I'm giving the principal a report."

I blinked, then looked at him. "I hear drug rings are a real problem here. Mexican cartel?"

He looked across the office at the receptionist. "No. They use idiot football players as mules to traffic their product."

I laughed.

"Most people don't recognize a sophisticated sense of humor like mine. Why are you here?"

"I'm here because I made a decision."

"First time for everything."

"Funny, funny."

"I wasn't joking."

I smiled. "You do know you're weird, right?"

"Yes," he said. "And I know you're an ignorant asshole. Weird versus ignorant asshole, weird always wins."

"I said I was sorry."

He shrugged and sat up. His fingers were long and slender, and he slowly tapped his knee with his middle finger. "And

20

I accept your apology. But that doesn't *not* make you an ignorant asshole."

I felt better for some reason. At least he was honest. "Fair enough. So, why are you really here?"

"My counselor thinks she needs to counsel me."

"About what? Your sophisticated sense of humor?"

"No. She needs to think she's doing her job, so I come twice a week. I don't like disappointing people, because I have an abnormal trait called empathy. Why'd you make a decision?"

I didn't know where to start with this kid, so I didn't. I slouched in my chair. "I don't know. Just tired of everything. Coach was busting my balls because I'm failing math, which means I can't play ball, which means it's a big pity party for him and my dad."

"Why're you failing math?"

I frowned, wondering why he was interested in the least important thing about this whole deal. "Because I suck at it," I said. I didn't want to talk about it, because of all the things I *could* do well, math truly wasn't one of them. It wasn't that I was slacking. The numbers just didn't fit in my head right. "So, who are the drug smugglers if they're not a Mexican cartel?"

"I was joking."

"Yeah, I know. It was a way to change the subject."

His eyes went to the clock. "Nine minutes thirty-seven seconds."

"What?"

He looked at the clock again. "How long I've been sitting here. I'll miss the bus."

21

"Where do you live?"

"Downtown."

The only people I knew who lived downtown were homeless, crazy, or drug addicts. "Huh."

He frowned. "Huh, what?"

"Where downtown?"

"The River's Edge."

"Where is it?"

He stared at me for a moment. "You *are* stupid, aren't you?"

"What?"

"Never mind. It's on the river between Maple and Monroe."

I wondered what this kid was all about. "I'm seeing my counselor, too. He's going to try and convince me to un-decision my decision, even though I'm not really sure what I decided. If you're done when I am, I'll give you a lift home."

He looked at me, and there was a shadow of caution in his eyes. "No thanks."

Mr. Reeves came out of his office, saw me, and motioned. I stood. "See you around," I said, then went inside.

5

I didn't know Mr. Reeves that well. He'd taken care of a few class changes for me, and overall he sort of came off as the kind of guy who didn't have much to say about anything. One of those ghosts in the hall who made an occasional appearance. "You wanted to see me?"

"Coach Williams called me after your meeting today. He's concerned."

I sat down. "I know."

He studied my face. "He relayed to me that he's worried about your attitude."

"No, he's not."

"He's not?"

"He could give a shit about my attitude."

He looked down at his desk, and I gave it a seventy-five percent chance that the next words out of his mouth would be for me to watch my language. No matter how rotten the core of the apple, keeping the outside bright and shiny was the most important thing. He took a breath, his eyes returning to me. "Then what is he worried about?"

My respect scale rose. Maybe he was cool. I hitched my head toward his door. "That glass case out in the office."

"The trophy case."

"It's the only reason I'm sitting in here."

He sat back. "Coach Williams told me you are failing math. That, to me, is a concern."

I laughed. "I suppose if me failing math were a concern, my math teacher would have called you. But he didn't. Coach did."

"Coach Williams also told me you've become . . . rebellious."

I looked around the room, searching for the usual signs. They were there. A poster of the basketball team. School colors on the walls. An old picture of him playing college football. Two framed newspaper articles from last year highlighting a win of some sort. I smiled. "You played ball?"

Satisfaction spread across his face. "Actually, I was a receiver for the Oregon Ducks back in the day. Second-string, but it was the experience of a lifetime."

"I'll bet," I said. "So, you're here to convince me to do what I need to do to put another trophy in your sacred little case, too."

The three-minute friendship we had disappeared, and his face hardened. "I think you're making assumptions, Mr. Patterson. Coach Williams—"

I stood. "Coach Williams is a douchebag, and I'm done talking," I said, then moved to the door.

"Yes, he is."

I turned back to him. "What?"

He nodded. "Yes, he is a douchebag. Will you sit down, please, Brett? I'm not your enemy here."

I gawked. "You do know that I could tell him you said that, right?"

"Coach Williams is well aware of how I feel about him. Yes, I played sports, but no, I don't care about that trophy case."

"Then why am I here?"

He gestured to the chair. "Why don't you sit down and tell me?"

6

I closed the door behind me. Preston was nowhere to be seen. I stood there for a moment, tempted to wait, when his counselor's door opened and Preston walked out. He looked at me. "What are you doing standing there?"

"I just got out."

He hitched his backpack higher on his shoulder and walked past me. "All the world's problems solved in twenty minutes," he said.

I watched him go, this kid who was silent but had so much to say, then followed him out. He exited the building and walked to the edge of the parking lot, where he stopped and stared at his watch.

I came up behind him. "You sure you don't want a lift?"

He turned. "Wow. I've got a fan club."

"I got a car is all. You said you'd miss the bus."

He looked at me. With those big wide-set eyes and small

nose and chin, he reminded me of a cartoon character. "Do you know why most people give to charities?"

I felt the warmth of the afternoon sun on my cheek. Mr. Reeves and I had had an interesting talk, and even though I still didn't know what decision I *should* make, I knew what decision I *was* making. "I don't know. To help people?"

"People help other people because it makes them feel better about being selfish."

"There are tons of people who are good."

He smiled for the first time since I'd met him. "I wasn't talking about tons of people. I was talking about you," he said, then walked away.

I'd never been a glutton for punishment, but I couldn't get the image of him sitting calmly with egg all over him out of my mind.

I watched him shuffle off, walking like a gangly duck, and went to my car. Get in, turn the ignition, put it in gear, drive. As I drove out of the parking lot, I couldn't help myself. I pulled up alongside him and rolled the passenger window down. "Okay, I'm selfish, and I do feel guilty, but I had no idea it was going to happen. Will you get in the car now?"

He kept walking. "Why should I want to make you feel better? Why would I even want to *know* you?"

I stopped the car, thinking. Then I pulled forward and leaned over. "You shouldn't. But maybe I want to know *you*."

That stopped him, and he faced me. "You want to know me?"

I rolled my eyes. "No, I'm not gay. And yes, I do. Now get in."

He did.

"Where's your place?"

He buckled up. "I'll show you. Just head to Monroe Street and go over the bridge."

I pulled away from the curb. "So, how'd the counseling go?"

He looked at the middle console, where a crunched-up McDonald's wrapper lay. Next to it was an empty Red Bull can. There were various bags and wrappers strewn about the floor. My car wasn't the cleanest, and the backseat was full of months-old crap, too. He picked up the wrapper and held it, staring out the window. "It went fine. I think she's doing well with it."

"She? With what?"

"The grieving process. She's following it precisely. Straight from the book."

I drove. "Did she lose somebody?"

"No. I did. The state wants to make sure I'm coping correctly, so I check in with her. The school is very concerned about my emotional well-being."

"Who did you lose?"

He picked up the empty Red Bull can, then began slowly scrunching the wrapper inside. "My dad. Six months ago. See, we're supposed to go through stages of grief. She thinks we're at stage four, which is depression and loneliness."

I glanced at him. He'd picked up an old straw and was idly folding it into the can. "She thinks?" I said.

He nodded. "Yeah. A couple weeks ago she moved out of the anger and bitterness stage."

"She? I'm confused. You're not grieving about losing your dad?"

"Of course I am. Just not the way she needs me to."

28

"Why don't you tell her that?"

He inched his hand toward a gum wrapper, hesitated, then picked it up. He rolled it into a ball. Into the can it went. "Why would I tell her? I don't need her help, and I don't feel like arguing about where I am in her process."

"Well, then tell her you don't need counseling."

"It's just a check-in. Like mini-counseling. I have a regular counselor. He thinks the same thing, though. I think they talk."

"I'm totally confused, Preston. You're seeing a counselor that you don't need, you go to the school counselor to help her with your grieving process, and it doesn't bother you at all?"

"Nope."

"Why?"

He stuffed a used napkin in the can, twisting and turning it in. "Because it gets me what I want."

I glanced at him. He was systematically cleaning my car. "What? A neurotic need to clean my car?"

He set the can down, self-conscious. "I have a compulsion to keep things in order."

"No kidding? I never would have guessed. So, what is it that you want?"

He looked out the window. "How did your counseling session go with Mr. Reeves?"

"It wasn't a counseling session. He just wanted to talk."

Preston shrugged. "Going to see a counselor to talk is called a 'counseling session.' It's the definition of it."

I sighed. "It went fine, except that when I get home, all hell is going to break loose."

"Why?"

29

I turned left on Monroe. "Because I know Coach Williams called my dad, and the shit is going to hit the fan."

"I have no idea what you're saying."

I took a left on Madison Avenue. "I'm thinking of quitting football."

"Why would you care if your dad was mad about that?"

I rolled my eyes. "You're kidding, right? It's just like if you quit school. Wouldn't your mom be mad?"

"No, but if she were, that's her issue."

I gaped. "She wouldn't be?"

"She's not the one going to school."

I took a breath, again not knowing where to go with that statement. "So, what you're saying is that my dad, who has lived through me for the last three years because he loves football more than life, shouldn't be upset if I quit? And he shouldn't be pissed that I'd most likely be giving up a scholarship that could eventually get me into the NFL?"

"I'm not saying he shouldn't. He could be if he wanted to, I suppose. But what does that have to do with you playing your game or not?"

"Well, I guess my world is different than yours."

He pointed to a parking lot for me to turn into. "Only because you want it that way."

I pulled into the lot. "Nothing is the way I want it."

"What if you told your dad that it was none of his business? What if you ignored everything he said? What would he do?"

I smirked. "You don't know my dad."

"Would it make you bad?"

"Bad?"

"Yes. Like, bad. Like, a bad person."

"I don't know, Preston. You lost me."

"How is it his business?"

I stared out the window. "He'd make it his business."

He studied my face with those big eyes, and it made me uncomfortable. "How?" he said.

"He just would."

He opened the door. "Thanks for the ride."

I glanced around the empty parking lot. Clinkerdagger, a fancy restaurant, stood off to the left. "You live in a parking lot?"

"No." He pointed. "There."

I gazed upward, and what looked like a fifteen- or twenty-story office building stood looming over the river. "I always thought those were office buildings."

"No. Apartments."

"Huge windows for apartments."

He grabbed his backpack, then quietly slipped the Red Bull can into a side pocket. "They call it 'luxury condominium living.'"

"Wow. What floor do you live on?"

He got out, then shut the door. "The top one."

7

I sat in the car, my head swimming. I didn't want to go in. I wished my dad was out, but since he worked from home, he was always there.

I thought about Preston and what he'd said. Or not said, but asked. That was the strange thing. He never really said anything; he asked everything. From being distracted by wrappers in my car to not understanding why anybody would be upset that I quit football, he confused me. What if I did tell my dad it wasn't his business? What would he do?

I turned the car off, hopped out, and walked up the driveway.

He was sitting at the kitchen table, reading the newspaper and drinking a beer. There wasn't a day after four o'clock when he didn't have a bottle in his hand. Our house wasn't big enough to hide in or for me to go to my room without him knowing I was there, so I did what I knew I should. "Hi."

He looked up. "Coach Williams called."

I leaned against the kitchen entry. "Yeah."

He set the paper down and took off his glasses. He was a big man, but not huge; I got my height from him. At six three, he was an inch taller than me. He didn't have the build of a football player, but back in his day, he was. A receiver, just like me. He'd been good—great, from what I heard. Got a full ride to Washington State University, then blew his knee out his first season. End of story. Now he was a business consultant. He looked at me. "I spoke to your math teacher. Not much for football players, but you'll be fine to play if you get the extra credit done," he said, then squinted at me. "And by the way, you're grounded for disobeying an order. Don told me what you did in his office."

Don was Don Williams, or Coach Williams. I rolled my eyes. Lucky me that they would have a bromance together. "Dad, he was totally out of line. I already talked to my teacher. I talked to Mr. Reeves. I did everything I was supposed to. There was no problem with anything. The guy just gets off on using his power to crap on people."

He put his glasses back on, then picked up the paper, talking to it instead of me. "We're five games into taking the championship, and you hold the key. Roger Silvia, the scout from UCLA, is flying up for Friday's game, and you know why. He wants to meet, and I arranged a get-together here on Saturday. I'm pretty sure he's coming with an offer."

I stood in the doorway, staring at him while he ignored me. Sometimes I think he literally didn't hear a fucking word I said. *What if you ignored everything he said? What would he do?* Preston's words came to me, and as I watched

Dad, I didn't know what to do. As far as he was concerned, I didn't get to have an opinion on what I wanted to do. I'd spent the day listening to one man hammering it into me, and now I was listening to another man treat me like I was a chess piece in his game of life.

Everything rolled around my head like a spinning bingo basket. "I didn't do anything wrong, Dad."

He took a swig of beer. "Keep your eye on the goal, Brett."

Anger boiled through me. "What goal is that? My goal or your goal?"

He stopped mid-swig, then laughed. "You keep this up and you'll be grounded for the rest of the year. Be a smart-ass somewhere else, huh? There are much more important things going on than how you feel about being put in your place. Quit whining and be a man."

I was tempted to grab that beer and shove it down his throat, but I didn't. I turned around and went to my room. Invisible things don't talk, so I didn't.

8

Football players wore their jerseys to school on game days, just like the cheerleaders wore their uniforms. Banners strung across the hallways supported and celebrated the team, and an electric air filled the school with an underlying hum of excitement. The Saxons would be kicking ass and taking names.

In the first five games of the season, we'd outscored our opponents by a total of fifty-three points. I'd caught twenty-one receptions, for over four hundred yards, and had scored six touchdowns. My high school career included more completions and touchdowns than any other player in the history of the school, and I was well on the way to holding a state record for yardage. We'd taken state last year, and if we took it this year, the consecutive wins would be the first in history for Hamilton High School.

I was a star.

Lance Killinger, our quarterback, caught up to me in the hall after second period. Killinger and I didn't like each other, and it was well known that we didn't. It all started when he was born. He came out of the hatch looking down on the world, and for however much he thought his crap didn't stink, it did.

But he could throw and I could catch, and no matter how much of an arrogant assclown he was, that's all that mattered to anybody. He was the kind of guy I'd be happy to never know, but we flowed together on the field like twins. He bumped my shoulder, looking at my T-shirt. "Where's the jersey, Stick? You forget it?"

I had four minutes to get to class. "No."

"You slacking? Skipping weights in the morning, no-showing at practice yesterday. What's your deal?"

"Been busy is all."

"You gotta represent, man. We're the kings of this school."

I kept walking. "Kings, huh? Is that right?"

"What's up your ass?" he said. "Big guy nervous about tonight?"

"Just heading to class, Lance. Nothing special."

"Yeah, sure. Heard a UCLA scout is going to be here. Wow for you, even though I can nail a dime at forty yards, and the only reason you're good is that I hit your chest every time."

I faced him. "You know what I've never told you?"

He met my stare, the challenge there. "What is that, Stick? You want to tell me something?"

I thought of everything I wanted to say but hadn't. What I wanted more than anything was my fist punching his face inside out. "I wanted to tell you that you're an awesome quarterback, and I know you're going to kill it tonight."

He paused, a question in his eyes. "Yeah, sure. You know it. West Valley equals big-time fail. They suck."

"You got it," I said, taking a quick left into my class.

Sixth period let out, and I hustled to my car. As I neared, I saw Preston standing next to it. He was staring at something at his feet. I took my keys from my pocket. "Hey. Here to finish cleaning my car out?"

He looked up. "Hi."

"What's up?"

"Nothing."

"You just stand around people's cars?"

He looked at me, unsure, his eyes wavering. Like he was nervous, but not. "I was wondering why you're failing math. You didn't answer me yesterday."

I almost laughed. Math. Okay. My life was turned upside down, there was a huge game tonight, and he was wondering about math. "Because I suck at it. I told you that."

He looked at me. "I suck at football, but at least I know why."

"Why, then?"

"Because I'm five feet six inches tall, I weigh one hundred and seventeen pounds, and I have a tendency to fall down when I run."

I stared at him, wondering where he'd come from, and why. "Well, I just suck at it. The numbers get all jumbled in my head."

"I could probably help you if you want."

"Why? I thought you didn't want to know me."

"Because I'm brilliant."

I laughed.

He cast his eyes down. "Cool. Anyway, good luck with the game. Bye," he said, turning and shuffling away.

"Jesus, Preston! I wasn't laughing at you!" I called to him. He kept walking. "I was laughing because you say shit that's just so out there. Stop! Come on!"

He did stop, then turned and faced me, his hands stuffed in his pockets, his shoulders slouched.

I pointed to the passenger door of the car. "Get in. I need my car cleaned."

His eyes brightened. "Really?"

I opened the door. "As long as you can stand the garbage, yeah, really."

As we pulled out of the parking lot, I checked my mirrors, then drove down 37th Avenue. "So, where are you from?"

"A womb."

"Okay . . . where are you from, as in where did you come from before you started at Hamilton this year?"

"Chicago. We moved here after my dad died."

"How'd he die?"

"He was murdered for seventeen dollars."

"I'm sorry."

Preston drummed his fingers on his knee methodically. "You didn't do anything."

"I know. I just am, though. Did they catch the guy?"

He shook his head.

"So, you'll tutor me?"

"Yes."

I smiled. "Cool. Thanks."

He looked at me, totally serious. "I don't want to be your boyfriend. It's not that way."

"Damn," I said. He fidgeted, eyeing a pop can. I could almost feel his need to clean. I laughed. "Go ahead, OCD boy. Have at it."

He picked up the can. "Being that you are alive today, your dad didn't kill you Tuesday night."

"I don't know what's worse. Being completely ignored or being stomped on."

Preston frowned as he stuffed the can in a fast-food bag. "Why is being ignored bad?"

I turned, heading downtown. "Because I'm not me to him. Or anybody. I'm what other people can get for themselves. Just like you said. Have you ever just had somebody completely ignore you?"

"Considering I still have egg on my backpack and the burn of being ostracized by my cooler peers is still hot in my belly, I would appreciate being ignored more often."

I realized then that even if I had an idea of how much he was bullied, I would never truly know what it was like, and I felt a stab of guilt. "That won't happen again if I'm around."

He reached into my console, scooping up a handful of change. "My gay stalker is going to protect me now. Yay. I'm saved."

"I'm just saying, you know? It was a crappy thing to do, and I guess I'm seeing things differently now."

He began separating the pennies from the rest of the change. "I don't need anything from you, Brett. I can take care of myself just fine."

I shook my head. "Yeah, like having guys like Tilly make you into a fool in front of everybody."

He turned those big eyes to me. "Is that what he did? Made a fool out of me?"

"Well, you got egg all over you."

He looked down and stacked the pennies. "I suppose the definition of 'fool' depends on what side of the line you're on."

He was right. "Tilly is the fool."

Preston stacked nickels. "It doesn't matter what he is. It matters what I am. What time does it start?"

"What time does what start?"

"Your game."

"Three hours. Game time is seven."

He continued organizing my change, so I took the long way. I figured if we took a drive in the country, he'd have my car spotless in no time, but I was just happy to have a drive-in maid. Ten minutes later, I pulled into the parking lot. "So, about the tutoring thing."

"Yeah."

I put the car in park. "This Sunday work?"

He nodded. "I'll have to check my schedule, but I think I'm free from around five in the morning until eleven or so at night."

He had a paper bag nearly full of trash, and the passenger side of the car was cleaner than it had ever been. "Cool. How about I meet you here at around one?"

He opened the door. "Sure. And good luck with your game tonight."

. . .

At six o'clock, my cell rang. I ignored it. Ten minutes later, it rang again. I picked it up, turned the ringer to silent, and put it back down. I sat in my car, sipping on a soda and looking out over the northwest part of the city. I'd been draining the tank for hours driving around, and I'd finally pulled over, hopping out and taking a leak over the bluff.

Dusk settled over the skyline, the sun below the horizon, and I sat as the pink glow of the sunset faded to nothing. I glanced at my phone. Seven missed calls. I knew each one was another marker on my headstone, but I couldn't answer. I wouldn't answer.

I thought about my dad. It had all started with playing catch in the yard. Then my first team. I remembered not being able to sleep the night before games I was so excited. I remembered knowing, deep down and almost like it was natural, that I was *good*. Nobody had to tell me. I knew. And it felt good to know I was good at something.

Then it began changing. All the praise from my coaches and other parents built up, and my dad thrived on it. I did, too. I loved the attention, and I loved the game, but there were expectations. By the time eighth grade started, high school coaches from around the city were contacting my dad, offering ways to slide around the districting rules to get me on their teams.

Once my dad saw a future in me, things changed drastically. When I was a freshman, our postgame celebrations of getting ice cream or pizza turned into reviewing tapes, going over the playbook, talking strategy. Reviewing tapes then turned into incessant replays, and soon enough I dreaded it. Good plays and great catches were skipped over, and my dad focused on every minuscule mistake I made.

By tenth grade, training schedules and food restrictions were posted on the refrigerator. Ice cream and pizza were a thing of the past. Playing catch in the yard was history. Weekly barbecues in our backyard with Coach Williams turned into two-hour sessions in the living room where my dad and he talked about me as if I wasn't there.

All those years of pushing. All those years of my dad telling me what I wanted and what I needed. All the years of punishments, all the times he'd gotten drunk and knocked me around because I wasn't good enough. Football was everything in his life, and fortunately for him, he had a son that could live his dream. But it wasn't my dream anymore. I felt like he'd snuffed it out along the way.

From up on the bluff, I could see Joe Albi Stadium in the distance. At six-thirty, the stadium lights blinked on. Half an hour till kickoff. I closed my eyes and I could hear and smell and see everything. The locker room. The echoing voices. The excitement. The muffled sound of the announcer's voice welcoming the crowd.

Coach Williams would come in and give his talk. Not really a talk so much as a sermon from the pulpit of the gridiron. He'd tell us a hundred percent wasn't enough. He'd tell us second place is loser's place, and this field, his field, was no place for pussies. He'd wind it up, his chest heaving, his face turning red, his voice a growl as he told us nobody, *nobody*, could stop us. That we were champions.

It was the one thing that Coach was awesome at. Pumping us up. Getting us ready to smash. Our opponents will not just lose; they will have their souls ripped from them. They'll feel what it's like to be crushed under the boot of the Saxons, and we'd make it happen. We're the rulers of this league, and there's nothing that will stop us. Each and every one of us, he'd say, would show the world what it meant to be the best.

I opened my eyes and looked at those shining lights making an oval around the stadium, and I laughed. No, Coach. We wouldn't. I wouldn't. I'd sit in my car and wait for the end of the world, because I was done with people telling me what I should do for reasons I didn't care about. I was done having people ruin the thing I loved the most.

At seven o'clock, I flipped the radio on, tuning in to the game. And for the next four quarters, I listened to the Saxons get their asses whipped.

9

I shut the car off in front of the house and picked up my phone. Seventeen missed calls and ten unread texts. Five from my dad, one from my coach, and the rest from the team.

I saw the curtains move, and in the next moment the front door opened. My dad stepped out, his frame outlined by the light from the living room. He stood there, his arms crossed over his chest. My shoulders tightened. I took the keys from the ignition, then got out.

As I reached him, he didn't move. He just stared at me in the darkness. "You do know what you've just done, right?" he said.

I took a breath. "I made my decision."

He uncrossed his arms, running his hand through his hair. "No, you didn't. You just screwed yourself, Brett. That's what you did."

"I screwed myself? Or did I screw you?"

"That's enough."

"What's enough? Does it matter what I think?"

He slurred his words. "Coach and I had a meeting after the game. Nobody knows what's going on. He told the scout you came down with food poisoning and couldn't play. Silvia still wants to meet tomorrow. Ten in the morning. Here."

"I'm done playing."

He clasped the sides of his head with his hands, looking up. "And I don't want to get up every fucking day and be a consultant, Brett! We do what we have to do, and you have to do this! You're better than I am. God gave you something. Do you understand that?"

"No. I don't."

He grabbed my shoulders, bringing my face close to his. "DO YOU UNDERSTAND THAT?"

The only thing I saw reflected in his eyes was himself. His drunk self. But I didn't feel like getting thrown against a wall or yanked down the hall to my room. "Sure, Dad. Okay. I understand."

10

Dad peeked his head inside my door. Sunlight streamed through the blinds. "Come on, Brett. He's here."

I turned my TV off, then threw the remote on the bed. It was the first time I'd skipped my morning run in three years, and I felt like shit about it. Like something was missing. As I stood, I glanced at myself in the mirror, wondering for the thousandth time if I really did want to quit.

I walked down the hall and into the living room. Mr. Silvia was sitting forward in the recliner, his forearms across his knees. He was younger than I was expecting. In his early thirties. He wore a UCLA Bruins polo shirt, had dark, perfectly trimmed hair, and smiled. My dad sat across the coffee table from him.

Mr. Silvia stood, extending his hand. "Brett, it's nice to meet you."

I shook his hand. "Nice to meet you, too, sir."

He nodded, then sat down. "Are you feeling better? Your coach let me know you had food poisoning."

I sat down. "Yeah. I suppose he did."

Silvia faltered, his face breaking from his smile for just the slightest second. "Hey, it happens to the best of us, huh? It doesn't matter, though. I've seen all your tapes, and honestly, your numbers stand alone. You're a fantastic player. Best I've seen in my entire career."

For all I sucked at math, numbers swam through my head. My records. How many trophies I had. How many touchdowns I'd scored. How much it would cost to go to a school like UCLA. All the things that mattered in my life. "Thanks."

He smiled again. "Great. Well, I'm not going to waste your time or mine." He leaned forward. "I know you're going to have other schools after you, but would you like to be a Bruin?"

I could almost feel the excitement emanating from my dad. I could see Mr. Silvia, sitting there acting like he was doing me the biggest favor of my life. I blinked, focusing on his face. I'd made the biggest, boldest statement of my life last night by not playing, and everybody was acting like nothing had happened. "No, sir, I wouldn't."

The silence of something dying filled the room. Mr. Silvia's lips parted, but he didn't speak to me. He looked at my dad. "Sir? Would you mind telling me what's going on? Has Brett accepted an offer from another school?"

I swear to God I heard my dad's heart constricting. He had to make himself breathe. After a moment, he spoke. "No, Mr. Silvia. UCLA is for Brett. As you know, it's my alma mater. This year has been a stressful time for him is all," he said, then smiled. "Call it cold feet, you know? All the attention, the newspapers, and now you. He's just nervous."

Mr. Silvia sat back, relieved. He looked at me. "No problem. I've seen it before, and it happens, Brett, but there's nothing to be nervous about. Have you seen the campus? It's great. Sunshine all year round, Southern California at its finest, and a fantastic football team with a tradition and history that you'll be a part of."

I stood. "Mr. Silvia, I really appreciate the offer, but I quit the team. I'm done playing football."

My dad frowned, his expression surprised. Almost like he hadn't listened to a goddamn word I'd said for the last two days. "Come on now, Brett. It's just been rough this year. I'm sure we can—"

Rage exploded through me. I stared at my dad sitting there like some broken hero pleading for another chance at something he'd never get. "Dad! Will you fucking listen to me? For once in my life, listen!" I yelled, feeling hot tears come to my eyes. "I QUIT! I'm done! I don't want to play!"

His mouth hung open. Mr. Silvia stood. "Brett, can we step outside for a moment? I promise I won't try to convince you of anything. Just a minute of your time."

I wiped my eyes on my sleeve, embarrassed and ashamed and sick all at the same time. "Sure."

Outside, Mr. Silvia took a card from his back pocket and looked at me. "This is none of my business, Brett. My job is to find great football players. That's all. If you're not that guy, that's fine. Take this card. Call me if you change your mind and we might be able to sort things out, huh?"

I looked at his outstretched hand and realized he was a good guy. Not a salesman, not a shark. I took the card. "I'm sorry about that. Things just . . ."

"Don't apologize, Brett. Just think about what you want."

I watched him drive his rental car away, then went back inside. Dad sat on the couch, his elbows on his knees, head in his hands. I shut the door. He grunted, looking at the floor between his feet. "You happy, son?"

"No."

"How could you do this?"

"Coach told me to choose a path to walk. I chose. You didn't listen. Nobody does."

He took a breath. Immense silence pounded the room in time with the beating of my heart in my ears. I'd done it. I'd taken my first steps down that road.

I stood there looking at him and I didn't know what to feel. I loved him. He was my dad. I remembered the first football he'd ever bought me. A cheap rubber Walmart ball that I slept with because he told me I was good at catching it. I was good at something, and the only thing that mattered was that he'd said so.

All the times when I was little that we played catch in the street. All the years when it was fun. Just him and me. Nobody else. Then it turned into something different. Endless criticism. Endless pressure. Some sort of future that I had no idea about. I blinked. "Remember when we used to play? Just us. Out in the yard? Why can't it still be that way?"

"Because you're not a little boy anymore. You're a young

man with a future you don't realize, son. And it's my job to guide you to it."

"When was the last time you told me I did a good job?"

He clenched his teeth. "Brett, for God's sake, aren't we past that? This is serious."

"I've got to go," I said. Then I left.

11

Sunday, Preston met me in the parking lot, and he brought a massive black eye with him. Still swollen, it looked like a split-open plum with a blood-red center. I shut the car door. "Whoa," I said, looking at him. "What happened to you?"

"I was doing recon when I was set upon by several criminals."

I smiled. "Back to the drug smugglers, huh?"

"Sure."

I couldn't stop looking at his eye. "You okay?"

He gestured to the building. "Want to come up? We can study in my room."

"Sure. Lead the way."

"Want to see a marvel of modern society's ability to waste money?"

"Sure. Why not."

He went to the car. "Get in. I'll show you."

I got in and fired up the engine, and he directed me through the parking lot to a garage door. He handed me a key card and told me to swipe it.

"Key in one, two, three, four."

I pushed the buttons, then handed him back the card. "That's original."

"My mom needs something simple."

Another mystery of Preston. I drew a blank when I tried to picture his mom. As the door opened, it revealed what looked like a parking bay, but there was no exit.

Preston picked up a ziplock bag with a crust of stale bread in it. "Turn the engine off. There are carbon monoxide sensors."

I did. In another moment, the door behind us closed. Lights came on, bathing the small space in fluorescent light. Then we moved. I jumped. "Whoa, what's this?"

"It's a car elevator."

"We're going up?" I said, looking around.

"Yeah. To my floor."

"Dude, you seriously have a personal car elevator?"

"Yes. It takes us up, then revolves, turning the car around for when you're ready to leave."

"Everybody has one?" I asked, feeling us moving upward.

"No. Just the top two floors. The peasants below us have a regular parking garage."

A minute later, we arrived. The car spun a one-eighty, then slid to the right, next to a gleaming BMW. Off to my left was a short hallway with a door at the end. I laughed. "That is so cool!"

He got out. "All my friends are impressed. Come on."

I looked at the car. "That your mom's?"

"Yeah. She's out with her new friends."

I followed him to the door, and he took me inside. We landed in the kitchen first, which was half as big as my whole house. Granite counters, a massive stainless steel refrigerator, two ovens, a huge island with a sink, barstools, shining pots and pans with copper bottoms hanging from the ceiling. I felt like I was on one of those shows where they tour famous people's homes.

Preston waved as he walked. "This is the kitchen. We never use it." He kept going, leading me to the living room. Floor-to-ceiling windows looked out over the city, with the river rushing by nineteen floors below. Leather sofas, chairs, tables, paintings, and lamps filled the room. All high-end. "Living room," he said.

I looked at the paintings. When I was little, I'd loved art class, and I'd even stopped by a gallery downtown a few times just to stare at all the different works. I recognized one of them now. A Monet. It was of a woman standing on a hillside of flowers, a parasol on her shoulder, and it looked like she was waiting for someone. I'd always wondered who. "Your mom into art?"

"No. Our old house had a Thomas Kincaid print over the mantel that she thought was pretty because there were hidden animals in it."

I stepped to the windows. "Awesome view."

He stood next to me. "Yeah. That's the best part. Sometimes at night I just stand and look out over the lights. Sort of like staring at fish."

"Fish?"

He nodded. "Clinically proven to reduce stress. You should try it."

"I don't have fish."

He led the way through the dining room, then down a hall. "Neither do I. Most doctors' offices do, though. Sick people are stressed."

"Yeah. Maybe I should go hang out."

We stopped at a door. He pointed to three more doors down the hall. "Guest room, master bedroom, study. This is my room." He opened the door, and I was greeted by a bedroom bigger than our living room. I'd expected more of the same fine furnishings, but I was surprised.

The room was almost entirely empty. A bed with no frame. A nightstand with a clock and a lamp on it. An old desk in front of the massive windows, chair included. On top of the desk was a computer. Next to the computer was a small CD player. Next to the keyboard was a smartphone with a pair of headphones plugged into it. Next to the desk was a mini-refrigerator.

I turned a circle, taking in the only other piece of furniture. A dresser. Four posters clung to the walls behind his bed, which faced the bank of windows looking over the city. All comic book posters. The Hulk. Captain America. Spiderman. Batman. "You like comics?"

"I collect them."

"Cool. I used to read *Superman*."

He pointed to a door, next to his closet. "Bathroom in there, if you need to go."

"Thanks," I said, studying his room. The posters were hung perfectly level, spaced evenly apart. His comics were in a neat pile on a shelf. His bed was made. Not a crease on it. The smartphone was placed in line with the keyboard, and the keyboard was centered perfectly in front of the computer. The headphones were rolled into a perfect circle. Not a wire or connection to be seen under the desk—unlike mine, which was a jungle of black vines.

Preston walked to the door. "I'll be back with an extra chair. There's stuff in the fridge if you want." Then he was gone.

I felt like I was in a normal earth room, but in a different dimension of almost neurotic, *Leave It to Beaver* organization. I could imagine June Cleaver flitting around the room with a duster in her hand. Everything was so neat, I felt like I shouldn't touch anything. I opened the fridge. Water, Mountain Dew, grape soda, Pepsi, and Sprite. All lined up perfectly. Then I noticed. Grape first. Mountain Dew second. Then Pepsi, Sprite, and water. All alphabetically organized.

I took a Mountain Dew, then walked to the bathroom door, opening it. I laughed. It wasn't a bathroom, it was a bathroom's bathroom. A walk-in shower with three heads. Next to that a jetted tub. Two sinks. The only normal thing was the toilet.

Feeling sneaky, I looked back into the room, then crept to the medicine cabinet, opening it. Yep. Everything perfectly placed, but this time in order of use.

"Did you need something out of there?"

I jumped, turning. "Sorry. I had to."

He looked at me. "Had to what?"

"Your room. It's, like, perfect. Everything. I had to see the bathroom."

"I like things orderly."

"Yeah. I feel like I shouldn't be here."

He shrugged. "You probably shouldn't be looking through my personal items, but no. I invited you here. Why don't we start?"

He sat at the desk, and I joined him while he booted up his computer. I took a swig of soda. "You mind if I ask a question?"

"Go ahead."

"You have the coolest place I've ever seen, but then we get to your room. It looks like mine, but just neat. Why? Does your mom not buy you good stuff?"

He fiddled with the mouse. "I like my old things."

"You weren't always rich?"

"No."

"How'd you get all the money?"

"My dad had a life insurance policy. Actually, he had four. My mom didn't know about them. They equaled over two and a half million dollars."

"Wow."

He stared at the screen. "So, what are you studying in math?"

"How'd you really get the black eye?"

He logged on to the Internet. "I had a confrontation last night."

"What happened?"

"I was punched in the eye. How did the game go?"

"I wasn't there."

The corner of his lip turned up in what could have been a smile. "I know. I was being facetious."

I didn't bother with not knowing what "facetious" meant,

because he was the only person I knew who would know what it meant. "This whole thing sucks, you know?"

"Yeah. Life sucks for everybody sometimes. What are you studying, Brett?"

"Algebra."

"Okay. Then let's start."

12

Preston spent an hour going over the basics of stuff that my teacher never really explained as easily as he did, and by the time we were done, I actually understood some of it. After I got in my car and took the elevator down, I sat in the parking lot for a few minutes. He really was brilliant. Weird, but brilliant.

He'd told me that everything in our existence came down to numbers.

I breathed a sigh of relief when I got home. Dad wasn't there. No note on the door, which meant he was still pissed. Fine. Let him be pissed. I hoped he was at the bar in Lincoln Heights, getting wasted enough that he'd stumble in later and pass out. I flipped the TV on and my phone rang. It was Mike. "Hey," I said, listening absently to the news in the background.

"Stick, what's up? Why the no-show at the game?"

I turned the volume down as the newslady rambled on about a carjacking attempt downtown foiled by a good citizen. I focused on Mike. Here it was. The big question. I knew it had been coming, and I knew it would come from Mike. "I quit the team."

Silence. Then laughter. "Okay, good one. You really sick?"

"No."

"You didn't wear your jersey to school Friday."

"I didn't."

"You visit with the scout yesterday?"

"Yeah."

"They offer you a scholarship?"

"Yeah."

"Awesome! Damn, I knew you'd get it. In the bag, man."

I flipped the TV off. "I didn't take it, Mike. I declined."

There was an awkward silence. "You're serious."

"Yeah."

"Why? Coach? Your dad? What happened?"

"I don't know. I'm just tired of it. Everything. It's not fun anymore."

"Dude, we totally got creamed last night . . . and all because you aren't having fun? What kind of chickenshit answer is that? Everybody relies on you, and you just bail on us?"

"Is that what you rely on me for, Mike? Winning games?"

He ignored the question. "Don't do this, Stick. We need you. We'll lose any chance at the championship if you quit."

"I guess so, then."

"You guess what? That you're screwing us over?" His voice rose. "That you're being a selfish prick?"

"So, the only reason we're friends is so you can win, Mike?"

I waited for an answer, but the only thing I got was a dead line. I stared at the TV, phone in my hand, my insides empty. Everything screamed in me that I was being selfish. Everybody needed me. Coach, my dad, Mike, the team. But why did they need me? For their own selfish reasons? Did they really want me to play because they gave a crap about me, or did they want me to play because I could get them something?

Just as much as I was screaming at myself for being so selfish, I knew the resounding answer was that they wanted me for themselves. For the game, for the win, for the trophies, and for the championship. Bragging rights. Bullshit. Everything that made me hate playing football was pressuring me to play football, and my best friend had just proved it.

I felt hollow.

I stood, walked to the kitchen, and opened the fridge. I grabbed a bottle of Coors Light and twisted off the cap. I took a long swig. Screw it. I'd had four beers in my life, and as far as I was concerned, I could have one now. No doubt my dad was huddled at the bar with Coach or his buddies talking about how they could bring me back into the fold. Get me back straight.

Preston was right. It was none of their business, and I knew the answers because I was standing in my kitchen drinking a beer alone. Everybody else was worried about themselves, and it was time for me to do just that. Worry about myself.

I tanked the beer, threw the empty in the trash, and grabbed another. I walked back to the living room. I felt the buzz, light and heady, and sat. Maybe my dad had the right idea, after all. I looked at my phone. One text message. I flipped it open.

Killinger.

It read: **Herd u quit. U set me up. See u 2moro for sure.**

I downed half the bottle, remembering what I'd said to Killinger in the hall Friday. With the beer skimming over my brain, I laughed. Fine, Lance, bring it on. I texted: **Thought u culd nail a dime at 40 yards.**

I flipped my phone shut and drank the rest of the beer. I went back to the kitchen, ditched the bottle, and grabbed another, which I downed before grabbing yet another. My phone buzzed. I flipped it open. Killinger. **Ur gonna pay for that.**

I laughed. **FUCK YOU,** I texted, feeling giddy. Stick Patterson didn't say things like that. Stick Patterson did what he was told. He worked, he worked harder, and he took it. He toed the line, followed the rules, and did what his daddy said to do.

For the team. My dad's mantra. I looked at the full beer. Drink it because it doesn't matter. Drink it because nobody can tell you not to. I held the bottle up, toasting my dad. "You want me to be you, Dad? Well, here's to me being you," I said, then swilled it down, my eyes watering, my stomach revolting, and my mind swimming. I gagged, then opened another and drank.

I stumbled into the living room and looked at the picture on the mantel. My mother. She died having me. When I was ten years old, I realized I had caused her death. When I asked my dad, he told me that she'd have done whatever it took to bring me into the world. She loved me.

She was pretty. An angel, really. Dad told me she held

61

me. She kissed me before they had to take me away. I was premature. I didn't think about her often, but sometimes I talked to her. When things were bad. When the world closed in and I felt like I had nobody.

I wondered what she'd say. If she was here now, what? Would she tell me to play? Would she tell me I was being selfish?

I stared at the picture. "What should I do?"

I stood at the mantel, my insides twisted, mind reeling, eyes blurry. "Why aren't you here? Why can't you be here?"

Silence. Nothing. No answers. There were never any answers.

13

"**W**ake up."

I opened my eyes, my mouth dry as cotton, my head pounding. The world spun. I blinked, looking around. My stomach turned. Empty beer bottles. Me on the living room floor. My dad glaring down at me.

"Get up."

A strong hand on my arm, pulling me.

"I said get up!"

He yanked, wrapping his arms around me and dragging me across the floor to my room.

His voice was rough. "You don't drink in my house, you stupid fuck."

I tried to focus, shaking the spins away. My words came slow, and it was hard to form them. "Only you can do that, right? Well, I'm you. Good job, Dad."

He slung me on my bed. I closed my eyes. I smelled beer on his breath. He leaned over me. "You're lucky I don't beat it out of you," he said, and the next thing I heard was my bedroom door slam shut.

14

I woke up to my alarm. Pain. My head pounded, and my stomach felt like it had a basketball stuffed in it. My muscles were stiff and weak. I looked over the side of the bed. A bowl filled with puke next to the bed said that my dad had come back in. Probably just to save the carpet. My stinking life in a nutshell.

I lay there, then turned on my back and stared at the ceiling. If I could stay in bed for the rest of my life, I would. Just be here. Without the headache. But no. Monday morning. I had to get dressed and train, and without thinking, I slung my legs over the side of the bed and looked for my running shorts.

With the dull roar in my head as a backdrop, I realized I had no reason to get up. I had an hour and a half before school. I was free.

I didn't feel free, though.

A few minutes later, I got up, thinking of the night before, with my dad standing over me. The look in his eyes. The hardness. It wasn't much different from the way it was after a game. I could catch for a thousand yards and the only thing he'd have to say was that I could have done better. That if I wanted to make it to the NFL, every little thing counted.

I remembered one time I took a short pass on our fifteen-yard line and ran for eighty-five yards, scoring the winning touchdown. On the way home, the only thing he said was that I should have tucked the ball deeper into my arm. Nothing was ever good enough for him.

I was like a machine to him. Tighten a bolt here and bang a hammer there and it would work better.

I showered, willing the hot water to rinse away the alcohol emanating from me. When I came out, he was in the kitchen, reading the sports section of the paper. I opened the fridge and grabbed the milk. I looked at it, and my stomach turned. I put it back and opened the cupboard and poured four ibuprofen from the bottle.

He turned the page of the paper. "I don't know what your problem is, son, but I'm not going to watch you let your future slip away."

I ran the tap, filled a glass, and swallowed the pills. "Or what?"

He stopped reading, then set the paper down, staring at me.

I rinsed the glass and put it back in the cupboard. I shook my head. It was useless. "I'm going to be late," I said, even though I was a half hour early. I walked to the front door,

66

picked up my bag, then went to grab my keys. They were gone. I looked under a stack of mail, then searched the floor.

My dad came to the living room entry. "I took your keys."

"Why?"

"Because you don't deserve them."

I clenched my teeth, my head pounding. "I paid for that car. It's mine."

"You want to talk about money, Brett? How much have I spent on your training? Your camps? You know how much it cost to send you over to Seattle every summer? It's money we don't have, but you get it. You get it all. And now you want to throw it all away."

It hit me right then that no matter how much somebody said they wanted something *for* you, there was always something they wanted *from* you. My dad was no different. "I didn't ask for any of it. I just wanted to play."

"I didn't raise a quitter," he said, then turned and walked away.

I got to school five minutes before class started. I had to run the last two miles to make it in time, and I was winded when I hit the front doors. I felt like I was in some sort of stupid high school movie. First one person, then another, then ten more, then everybody in sight stopped what they were doing and stared as I walked down the hall. Word traveled fast. The quitter had arrived.

I tried to make myself not care, but I couldn't. My shoulders tightened, my stomach turned, and the headache I had woken up with returned, throbbing like a massive gong in my brain.

I kept my head down and walked upstairs to my locker. I sighed when I saw it. Somebody had scrawled "STICK THE PRICK" on it with black marker. Instant humiliation coursed through me. I heard several people laugh as they saw me read it, and I wished I was dead.

I stared at the words, my heart hammering, and took a breath. This was me. I'd made the decision, and this was only another reminder of why I hated playing football. But I had something to do, and I intended to do it today.

I saw him at lunch. He was leaning against his car, a bag of chips in his hands, talking to Kim Wayans. I walked up to them. "Hey, Mike."

He looked at me, and his expression was hard to read. "Hey, Stick."

I smiled at Kim. "Mind if I talk with Mike for a minute?"

She giggled. "Big-guy-football-player talk?"

I gave my best fake grin. "Yeah. Something like that," I said, then watched her walk away.

Mike tossed the bag of chips on his hood and crossed his arms. "You blew it, man. You so blew it."

I shrugged.

He looked at me. "Are you, like, dying of some disease or something? Because otherwise, I can't figure out what the fuck you're doing."

"We've been friends for over five years."

"Yeah. Five years of win," he said sarcastically.

"That's all I am to you, then." I fumed when he didn't

answer. Why answer when the truth was the truth? Even so, it pissed me off even more. "I guess if I were like you, we wouldn't be friends, Mike." I stared at him. "I mean, why would I want to know a second-rate lineman? A fucking average no-name nothing with a number on his back."

"I'm not second-rate."

I knew he wasn't. He was a great player, and I was hurt. There'd been this thing in the back of my mind that he of all people, out of everybody, would come through for me. That he would accept it. Accept me. I calmed myself down. "I know. I'm sorry. I just figured you'd see it different."

He rolled his eyes. "Well, it's sort of hard to. So much is riding on it, you know?"

"I've lived for this game, for my dad, for the team, for Coach, and for everybody except me since I was twelve years old, and I'm done. They make this game ugly, and now you're doing the same thing. You're my best friend, and all I get from you is shit. Not one single person has even asked me why."

"Why would they ask? You're the best. You got what everybody wants, and you've obviously gone crazy." He paused, then shook his head and lowered his voice. "You got a shot at something I don't, Stick. Don't you get that? No matter how hard I try, I'll never be good enough to go pro. And you're letting it go. That's crazy."

Mike worked harder than any other player on the team, and he was good. But he was right. He *didn't* have what it took to go pro. But I knew that if we took state again, he'd have a chance at some decent scholarships. I squinted. "You've got a shot at a scholarship, huh?"

He said nothing.

"What school, Mike?"

"U of I. If I keep my stats up and we take state, I could get a free ride. Don't you see, Brett? It's not just you. It's me, too."

"Yeah, I see, Mike," I said, deflated. Was there anything real in this world? Mike and I were *best friends*. We'd told each other our deepest secrets. Our dreams. We'd shared our lives like brothers, and it had all been for one thing. His stupid fucking scholarship.

"No, Stick. You don't see. I know what you're thinking, and maybe it's true. But you know as well as I do that I'll never get into a decent college without this. You know our situation."

I did. Mike's father was long gone. Last he'd heard, his dad was in prison in Kentucky serving a sentence for drug dealing. His mother made just enough money to keep them in a decent house in a decent neighborhood, but her credit was shot. He'd looked into student loans, but with his grade point, the most he would be able to do would be community college. "I get it, Mike. I do," I said, then walked away more confused than ever.

15

I slogged through the rest of the day pretending I was invisible, which wasn't too hard because people treated me like I had a rare strain of the bird flu. Half the guys I saw from the team didn't even look at me. The bonus was that I didn't see Coach.

Preston was supposed to meet me at my car for tutoring at his place, but since my most awesome dad had taken my keys and I was on foot, I missed him. I didn't have his phone number, either, which sucked, so I hopped the bus downtown, walking to his place in hopes that he was there.

I walked around his building till I found the lobby and got buzzed up to the top floor. When the doors opened, I found myself in a small waiting area with two chairs. I knocked on the door to the apartment, and a few seconds later a man answered. I blinked, wondering who it was, since Preston's dad was gone. "Hi. Is Preston home?"

The man, dressed in a suit and with his tie loosened, stared at me. He was shorter than me, around forty-five years old, with a drum for a stomach. He had startling blue eyes and dark close-cut hair, and he wore a class ring on his right hand. Most times I try not be judgmental, but some people were born with asswipe smeared all over their faces, and he was one of them. He studied me for a moment before answering. "No."

I looked back at him, weirded out by his stare. "Do you know when he'll be home? We were—" I said, but he cut me off, calling back over his shoulder.

"Diane, your kid has a friend at the door."

By the way this guy was acting, the first thing that came to mind was the black eye Preston had had yesterday. I nodded. "I can come back later. No problem." But then I heard shoes clattering across the marble entry.

Preston's mom wasn't what I imagined. She was dressed in a light blue silk blouse and a pair of those super-expensive jeans laced with white stitching. She had highlighted blond hair and wore too much makeup. My first impression was that she was a fifty-year-old woman doing everything she could to not be fifty. It wasn't overboard, but she easily fit into the cougar category. She looked me up and down, then smiled. "You're one of Preston's friends?"

Her eyes were kind. Warm. I nodded. "Uh, yes. He's helping me with math, and I missed him at school," I said, not adding that the reason was that my dad had stolen my car.

She held her hand out, smiling again. "Well, I'm Diane, Preston's mother. And you are . . . ?"

"Sti—" I began, then stopped. "Brett Patterson."

72

The man's eyes widened. "Stick Patterson? Of the Saxons?"

I nodded. "Yes."

He smiled, his face opening up like a jack-o'-lantern. "Well, damn, come on in! I didn't figure that kid had a friend in the entire world, and now I've got the best receiver in the state standing here."

Diane looked down and wiped her hands on her jeans. Then she took a breath. "Yes, Brett, please come in. It's nice to meet one of Preston's friends."

I followed them to the living room, and Preston's mom showed me to a leather loveseat. The man sat across from me in a matching leather recliner. He slapped the arm, shaking his head. "Stick Patterson," he said again, grinning. "You know, I went to Hamilton years ago. Played ball, too. Great school. Best in the city. By the way, the name is Tom. Tom Clarkston. I'm an attorney." He winked at me. "If you ever need anything, you just call me up."

Preston's mom offered me a glass of water, which I accepted. "Thank you." I wondered how many ambulances Tom had chased in his career.

Preston's mom sat on the other couch. "So, how long have you and Preston known each other? I'm afraid he's not much of a talker."

I felt like I was being interrogated, but nicely. "A little while. We met in the guidance office. I'm horrible at math, and he's really smart. Actually, like a genius or something."

Tom crossed his ankle over his knee, fiddling with the leather tassel on his shoe. "So, Stick, tell me about the season. It looks like you'll nab the title again. Great team, great team. Even read you might have some scholarships coming your way." He nodded like he was going to endow me with some sort of old-guy wisdom. And of course, he did. "You just be picky, huh? To be the best, you've got to go with the best. Definitely stay West Coast, though," he said, then leaned over and patted Preston's mom's knee. "Better-looking women, you know?"

I drank the water, remembering that Preston and his mother came from Chicago. "Thanks," I said, then looked at Preston's mom. "You don't know where Preston is, then?"

Tom straightened his neck, glancing at Diane with a glint in his eye. "Didn't he say something about playing with his little comic book things?" He grinned at me. "Hey, Stick, you still play with dolls?"

Diane cleared her throat. "Tom, please."

He nodded. "Fine, Diane, but you know how I feel about it. It's just not normal. What is he, fifteen? And he still pretends? Hell, I was working at a burger joint and smashing offensive linemen into the turf when I was his age." He winked again, smug and satisfied. "Defensive lineman. I was the guy going after your quarterback."

I wondered what it would be like to hook a car battery to his testicles and pull the switch, and I could easily imagine that Preston hated his guts. "Yeah, I've heard that's what defensive linemen do."

"You know, I've got a thousand dollars on the Saxons winning this week. Pretty big money, huh?"

"That's awesome, sir." I gave him a nod. "In fact, if I were you, I'd put two thousand on it."

He slapped the arm of the recliner again. "That's what I like. Confidence. I'm going to do just that."

I turned to Preston's mom. "I'd better get going. Could you tell Preston I stopped by?"

She stood, smiling at me. "Yes. And it's nice meeting you, Brett. Maybe we could have you over for dinner sometime?"

"Sure. That sounds great." I walked to the door.

Tom called out from the living room, "You take care of those hands, boy. They're golden!"

16

My dad was sitting in one of the chairs on our front porch when I got home. It was a bit after five. A half-empty beer sat on the little table next to him, and he held a football in his hands.

I walked up the steps. "Hi."

He stared at the lawn. "You said you missed playing catch. Like we used to."

"Yeah."

He stood and tossed me the ball. "Well, then, come on. Let's play."

It took a second for me to register that he was serious, but when I did, I brightened. He'd listened. Finally. I set my pack down and we spread out on the grass, just like we used to. Start close to warm up, then move back farther and farther. He lobbed the ball to me, stretching his arm. "How was school?"

I threw it back. "Weird."

He took a step back, throwing me a wobbly spiral. "Figured it would be."

I caught it, the skin of the ball warm in my hands. We'd do this after school all the time before things got serious. Just him and me, throwing and catching and talking. I threw. "Yeah."

He caught the ball and spun it in his hands. "You see Coach?"

"No."

He threw, this time harder, a true spiral. The ball felt good in my hands, and suddenly a twinge of remorse coursed through me. I loved football. "I don't know if I want to see him." I took a step back, throwing.

He caught it. "I know. It's hard to face people when you're ashamed," he said, then threw.

I felt the grain of the leather and gripped the ball tighter. "I'm not ashamed, Dad. I'm like a black sheep at school now anyway, so it doesn't matter. It's done." I threw him a lollipop pass.

He caught it, then took a step forward. "What's your plan now? Graduate, get a job?" he said, unwinding and throwing me a nail.

The ball hit my hands just like it should, the shock running up my forearms. "I don't know. Probably. Maybe I can enroll in community college. I've always liked art, you know? Remember that gallery downtown I used to go to?" I said before taking a step back and throwing.

He caught the ball. "So, you've dropped every plan you've had since you were twelve years old, and you don't know what you're going to do." He took another step forward, preparing to throw. "Is that smart?" He really unwound this time, giving me a bullet from ten yards away.

I clenched my teeth, and threw the ball back.

He threw it back, harder than before. His eyes were flat, his expression stone-faced. "You having a good time, Brett? This fun?"

I caught it. "Yeah, Dad. Great time." I jetted the ball to him, and it hit his chest as he caught it.

He took a stance, the ball in his hands and up by his ear. "You might want to get that job first, because . . . ," he said, then unleashed another bullet at me, "I'm not paying for a single thing you do from now on."

I caught the ball easily, but it was way too hard for how close we were. I realized we weren't playing catch. Not the way I thought we were. "I didn't ask, did I?" I said, throwing him the ball.

He caught it, glowering, his eyes intense. "This is what it's about, right? Just having some fun. Everything should just be fun," he said, then put everything in it that he had. The ball flashed toward my head.

They didn't call me Stick for nothing, I thought, laughing to myself as the ball slapped into my hands. I looked at him, at the other side of the yard, and knew things had changed between us. But I was pissed. I felt like screaming my lungs out at him or crumpling to the ground in a heap of tears. I took a breath, staring at the grass at my feet and feeling like I was trapped. Fine. He wanted it? He'd get it. I lifted my chin, staring at him. "That all you got, Dad? You might be a washed-up football player, but I didn't think you were washed out," I said, then tossed him the ball underhand.

He stood there, his chest heaving. I'd never seen the look in his eyes before. "You watch your mouth, Brett. You watch it."

"What? You don't like the truth? You couldn't hack it, could you? You could never be what you wanted, so you tried to make me be it. Well, you know what? I *am* better than you, and I'm not going to spend my life drinking myself to sleep every night because I live a life I hate."

The ball flew from his hand like a bolt of lightning, just like I knew it would. I didn't raise my hands. Just stood there, staring at him. The ball slammed into my chest like a torpedo, and the air exploded from my lungs. Pain shattered through me, but I stood there, my eyes never leaving his, my arms down. He took a halting step forward, coming toward me, the look in his eyes softening. Then he stopped, the ice returning. I felt like I was going to pass out.

He shook his head and began walking to the house. "There you go, Mr. Man. There you go."

I sucked in a breath of air. "I'm never going to catch another ball again," I called to him.

He didn't answer. Didn't look at me. Just went inside and slammed the door shut behind him.

17

In the bathroom, I pulled my shirt up and looked at the bruise. It was already turning a sick shade of purple. It looked like I'd been kicked by a mule. Every time I took a deep breath, shooting pain hit my chest, spreading through my lungs and around my rib cage.

I stood there, staring at myself. The game. All the times he'd made me wash his car or dig weeds out of the garden after I had missed a pass. *Hard work pays off, son. Remember that*, he'd say. *The only reason I'm making you do this is to show you what happens when you waste your talent. You want to wash cars for the rest of your life? Be a loser? I didn't think so. Think about that.*

Then he'd walk back into the house and crack a beer. Do as I say, not as I do, I thought. I shook my head, lowering my shirt. The fact was that I had no idea what I wanted to do other than football. I'd never had time to figure out anything other than the playbook.

I walked into the living room, glancing at the clock. Ten-fifteen. Dad was snoring in his recliner, the television news droning on about some vigilante in the city. Crime was rampant in Spokane, and people were getting fed up. I clicked the set off and stood in the middle of the room, looking around.

Screw him.

If I was my dad and I was going to hide a set of keys, where would I hide them? I looked at him sleeping. Then it hit me. He *wouldn't* hide them, because Stick Patterson would never even *think* of doing the unthinkable.

I walked into his bedroom, and there, right on the dresser, were my keys. I stared at them for a moment, then took them. For some reason, they felt lighter than they ever had. As I turned to leave, I glanced at myself in the mirror. *Stealing now, you idiot?* When I looked, I saw me. The same person I'd looked at every day since I could remember. Brownish blond hair cut tight. A decent tan. White teeth. Nothing stunning or Hollywood about me in the least, but not ugly as a stone. A person among billions, I thought. But now I was different. Stick Patterson didn't exist anymore. Brett Patterson did.

And he was stealing his own car.

I drove to drive, hitting the Palouse Highway and winding my way through the midnight wheat fields on the outskirts of town. It felt good to be going, even if I had nowhere to go. An hour later, I drove from the valley and entered the downtown core, aimlessly circling among the one-way streets. I passed the bus station and noticed a few guys standing outside under a streetlight, smoking and talking. They all stared as I passed.

The core was almost a ghost town this late on a week-night, and I headed west before turning right onto the Monroe Street Bridge. As my lights cut through the river mist that was flowing over the concrete railing, with the water below roiling over the falls, I saw a figure up ahead. I slowed as I neared.

He stood on the ledge, the river rushing a hundred and fifty feet below. A strong breeze would take him over. A jumper. Suicide. He wore a hoodie, had a small backpack on, and held his arms out like wings. As I passed, he turned his head toward me.

Preston.

I hit the brakes, put the car in park, and got out in the middle of the street.

He stared at me, his face shadowed by the hood over his head, reminding me of death. I shut the door. "What are you doing?"

Standing on the six-inch-wide barrier, he pointed. "You should turn your hazards on. People don't expect cars to be stopped in the middle of the lane."

His mom's boyfriend, who I was almost sure had given him the black eye, flashed through my mind. "Don't jump, Preston. Please."

"Don't jump where?"

"Off the bridge. Don't. Just get down."

Mist coiled around his feet in the darkness, and he lowered his arms. "Why would I jump off the bridge?"

"I don't know, but don't do it," I said, my mind scrambling for the right words. "Nothing can be that bad. Come on, just get down."

"You think I want to kill myself?"

"Well, you're standing on the railing of a bridge like you want to jump."

"If I wanted to kill myself, I wouldn't be talking to you. I'd be jumping."

"Then why are you—" I began.

He cut me off. "You never do anything dangerous, do you?"

"If you mean like standing on the railing of a bridge, no, I don't."

He looked down at his feet, then started walking, slowly placing one foot in front of the other like a tightrope walker. "Most people never do."

"You get a thrill from it, then?" I said, walking beside him.

He ignored me. "I'm not talking about standing on the rail, Brett. I'm talking about life. Most people do the same thing every day, but they don't do it because they like it. They do it because they're afraid to do anything else. It's dangerous."

"Maybe."

He stopped walking, then hopped down from the ledge. "You hungry?"

"What?"

"Food. Eat. Hungry. Are you?"

Twenty minutes later, we were sitting in the parking lot of a Taco Bell, chowing down on burritos from the all-night drive-through. I took a swig of Mountain Dew. "Why were you up there?" I asked.

He took a bite, chewed slowly, swallowed, wiped his

mouth with a napkin, and folded it neatly on his lap. "I always thought fear was a good reason not to do something. It's not, though. Usually it's the opposite."

"Like being afraid of the dark?"

He looked at me. "I'm not talking about irrational fear. I'm talking about real fear."

"What's real fear, then?"

I noticed a deep scratch above his eyebrow. His black eye had turned purple. He took a sip of his soda. "Why didn't you do anything when your friends egged me?"

"Because I'm an idiot."

He shook his head. "You were afraid. Of what would happen to you and your life and where you fit into it if you did something to stop what was wrong. We're conditioned to be afraid to stand alone." He smirked. "Contrary to what you might think about me and my pitiful and lonely life, Brett, I believe that most people are good. They're just afraid to do what they know is right."

"Your dad must have been really cool, huh?"

"Yeah. Why do you say that?"

"Because he must have taught you that."

Silence followed, almost a full minute as we sat in the dark. His voice came soft and low. "Have you ever hated something so much that you'd do anything to get rid of it? That you'd kill it if you could?"

I bit my lip, furrowing my brow. Tom, the boyfriend, came to mind, and I wondered if Preston was talking about him. "What are you saying, Preston?"

"When my dad and I came out of the museum that night six months ago, a guy walked up to us and pulled a knife.

I just stood there. I was so scared. I didn't know what to do. He told us to hand over our wallets, which my dad did, all the while begging the mugger not to hurt us. Then the guy told me to hand mine over. I couldn't move, so the guy moved toward me. My dad stepped between us."

I saw them there. Saw Preston's dad protect his son. Saw the knife flash, sinking into his chest. I saw a dead father on the sidewalk, his son kneeling over him, and I shuddered. "You hate the guy who killed him that much?"

"No."

I looked over at him in the dim. "Who, then?"

"I couldn't move, Brett. I wanted to, but I couldn't. Just like always. I could never do anything."

"It's not your fault, Preston."

"My dad died because I am what I am, Brett."

I looked at him. "No."

He stared at his hands, clenching them. "Most people get a chance to fix what they hate about themselves. Nobody gets killed." He glanced at me. "They just quit the team or switch schools or find new friends or get grounded, and they try to change. Nobody dies. Nothing is taken away forever."

Tears welled in my eyes, and I felt like the biggest loser idiot in the world. I thought about that day with Tilly and the eggs. The first time I'd noticed Preston. They didn't know what they were doing. Just a prank. Just some eggs. No harm, no foul, except that the kid they did it to was in more pain than any human being I'd ever known. The world had taken a shit on him, and the clouds just kept gathering, raining and raining in a torrential downpour of crap. I fought back my tears, feeling the warmth of rage course through me. "You can't do that to yourself, Preston. It's not your fault."

He folded the rest of his burrito up neatly, placed it in the plastic bag our food came in, and held it out to me. "You want the rest? I'd better go."

I took it, studying his face. He opened the door, got out, and walked away, and as I watched him go, my appetite disappeared with him.

18

When I got home, my dad was still snoring in the living room. I looked at the keys in my hand, trying to decide what I should do with them. Fear. Fear to do the right thing. I realized then that I was petrified of my father. Then I thought of Preston, and with a twinge of guilt I realized I was jealous of his relationship with his father. Even if he was dead.

I went to bed, and I decided right then I wouldn't steal from myself anymore.

19

I left early, before he woke up, and drove to school. Word was finally all the way out that I'd quit. No, I hadn't just quit—I'd ruined the team. I was single-handedly responsible for life on the planet ending. Three guys told me Killinger was going to kick my ass at some point, and I took it for what it was.

Serious.

After school, I walked across the grounds toward the gym. The longest walk of my life. I carried my helmet under one arm, my uniform under the other, and my heart in my throat. I'd waited in my car, thinking about it for a good couple of hours. Turning in the red-and-white uniform, I knew, was the last and final straw. There'd be no going back.

As I got closer to the doors, Lance Killinger and Tilly Peterson came out. My stomach shriveled.

They both stopped when they saw me. There were no

smiles. I kept walking, my eyes straight ahead, my chin up. I had quit for a reason, it was a good reason, and I wasn't going to be afraid of it. I also knew what would happen now, which was me getting my face beaten inside out. I kept my eyes straight forward, and as I passed them, Killinger side-stepped, shoulder-checking me into Tilly. When I hit Tilly, he shoved me back in the only way Tilly knew how. Hard.

My ass hit the ground, my helmet skittering away as I braced against the fall. Both guys stood over me in the deserted courtyard. Killinger smiled. "You always thought you were better than everybody else. Now we'll see."

"You're gonna be my bitch for the rest of the year," Tilly said.

I looked around, and through the glass doors of the gym, I saw Coach. He was standing there, watching. He did nothing. I reached for my helmet, and Killinger kicked my hand away. "You don't deserve it, man. You don't deserve those colors." He ripped the uniform from me and held it up. "Number seven. The great Stick Patterson," he said, then spit on it. Tilly laughed.

The next thing I knew, a slender arm reached down from over my shoulder. I turned my head, and Preston bent next to me, offering his hand.

Tilly and Killinger stared at the kid like he was insane. They'd been intent on me and hadn't seen him walk around the corner. I shook my head. "No. Go." One person getting his ass kicked was always better than two, and at least I could fight back.

Killinger laughed. "Look at this. Patterson has a new friend. Little faggot boy. You like eggs, faggot boy?"

Preston ignored them. He stared at me, and I saw complete and absolute fear in his eyes, which surprised me. In an instant, I understood everything he'd said the night before. About being afraid to do the right thing. I took his hand. He helped me up.

Tilly laughed. "Looks like you got some backup, Stick."

"No. Just you two and me. He stays out of it."

Preston picked up my helmet.

Killinger held his hand out. "Give it here, kid."

Preston stood, pale and silent, unmoving, his big eyes on Killinger.

"You want more than eggs this time, you fucking fag?" he said, stepping closer to Preston. They stared each other down for a few seconds, and Killinger grabbed Preston's arm.

Then it happened.

Preston swung the helmet with all his might, nailing Killinger square on the cheek. Blood sprayed. But it didn't stop there. He was like a tornado, arms flailing, the helmet a blur as he went after the falling Killinger.

As Killinger fell, Tilly rushed in and wrapped his arms around Preston, lifting him like a child. Preston was screaming. No, not just screaming, but from the bottom of his soul yelling bloody murder.

Skinny arms swinging, legs kicking, body thrashing in Tilly's huge arms, Preston fought uncontrollably, beating both Tilly and himself with the helmet. The helmet caught Tilly square in the face, and blood gushed from his nose. Preston, with spittle and slobber flying from his mouth like he was possessed by a spastic demon, lowered his chin and sank his teeth into Tilly's forearm, his yells turning to growls as he gnashed his teeth.

Tilly tried to control him, squeezing him tighter, but Preston was an animal, gnawing on his arm, hitting and kicking even harder. Tilly let out a painful grunt, lifted him higher, and body-slammed him to the ground.

It all happened so fast, I couldn't do anything, and I blinked when Preston's body hit the concrete. I heard the hollow thud when his skull hit. This didn't happen. People didn't do this. I'd never seen a situation so out of control.

The screaming stopped with the impact, and Preston lay still. Tilly, in a rage, leaned down, drawing back a giant fist to punch his head. I leaped at him, winding back and landing a massive haymaker against the side of his face.

I thought for sure I'd knock him out, but Tilly only roared in pain, backing off and holding his cheek. "Kid's fucking mental, man! Look at my arm!" He gaped, holding it up and watching the blood stream down.

I stood over Preston, staring at both Killinger and Tilly. Killinger looked like he was in shock, which he should have been. A hundred-and-seventeen-pound fifteen-year-old kid had just beat the shit out of both of them. "Leave, Lance. Get out of here."

And they did, with Tilly pointing at me and telling me I was finished, and that he'd finish me himself. Then it was over. I glanced through the gym doors just in time to see Coach disappear from sight. No other teacher had seen a thing.

Preston regained consciousness. He lay on his side in a fetal position, his face buried in his arms, his body heaving. He was talking to himself quietly through his sobs and moans, and the only thing I could understand was him mumbling "Sorry" over and over again.

I knelt down next to him, hoping to God he was all right. Tilly had slammed him hard. Too hard. "Hey, you okay?"

He didn't answer me. He was still heaving, still talking to himself, almost as if he was dreaming, still curled up like a wounded animal. I put my hand on his shoulder, and he flinched. "Don't touch me. Never touch me," he rasped.

I moved back, holding my hands up, palms toward him. "Preston, it's okay. It's fine. It's me. I'm not going to hurt you. I promise."

His whole body trembled. His face was smeared with blood and snot. He looked at me, those impenetrable eyes so deep and full of mystery and misery and sadness. He sat up, wrapping his arms around his chest. "Don't touch me."

"I promise I won't. Are you okay?"

His eyes were closed. His chin quivered, and he clenched his teeth, trying to calm the sobs coursing through him. "Leave me alone. I'm supposed to be alone, so leave me alone."

I didn't budge. For all I knew he'd cracked his skull. "Are you okay? Are you hurt?"

He blinked his eyes open, then got to his feet. "I'm supposed to be alone, Brett. Don't you understand that?" Then he got up and ran, his legs wobbly, his awkward body somehow not falling.

20

I knocked on the office door five minutes later, and in a moment, Coach opened it. I held my uniform, with Killinger's spit on the jersey, and my helmet, streaked with drying blood. He looked at them, then at me, his face a rock. "You lost us that game, Brett."

"You watched the whole thing."

"You've let so many people down," he said. "I thought you were better than that." It was as if he hadn't just witnessed a kid getting slammed into the ground hard enough to knock his brains out.

My stomach turned. How could I have ever listened to him? Respected him? How could I have ever believed that he was someone to look up to? "Tilly could have killed him."

If there was an emotion behind his face, God himself couldn't have dragged it out.

"You don't care, do you? It's all about your game, and

whoever doesn't play doesn't matter, huh? All about winning, no matter what you do to people." I dropped my helmet. It bounced on the floor, echoing through the empty gym.

His voice was low, full of gravel. "Don't quit, Brett. You'll regret it for the rest of your life."

A wave of revulsion shuddered through me as Preston's head hitting the concrete flashed through my mind. "You think I'd play for you? You're a shitty human being," I said, and then I flung the uniform at him.

He flinched, raising his hands to catch it.

I glared at him. "You suck. And you know what? You're nothing but a third-rate coach who has to play dirty to win."

21

My dad had called me four times during the day, leaving messages. The first two were threats about the car; then it turned to "I want to talk"; the last was nothing but him pleading for me to rethink quitting the team. I didn't call him back.

After leaving the gym, I headed to the parking lot. In the late-afternoon sun, my rear window glistened and sparkled, the glass spiderwebbed. A brick lay embedded in it. As I stared, I noticed the driver's door. Somebody had keyed it with a big X. A parting gift from Killinger and Tilly, no doubt.

It took me ten minutes to take out the broken glass. Thousands of brilliant pebbles covered my backseat. I left the brick in the parking lot and headed to Preston's place.

When I reached the lobby, I buzzed the apartment, and Preston's mom's voice came through the tinny intercom. "Yes?"

"It's Brett. Preston's friend."

"I'll be down in a moment. Please wait."

I stared at the walls until the elevator dinged, and when the doors opened, Preston's mom came out. She was dressed like she was going out for the night. Short skirt, cleavage showing, hair curled, makeup done. Her face, however, didn't look happy.

Her eyes were blue, and I noticed they were shaped like Preston's. She nodded, smiled briefly, and pursed her lips. "What happened?"

"I'm not sure I know what you're talking—"

She cut in. "What is going on with Preston, Brett?"

"I don't know, ma'am. Is he here?"

"Yes, he's here. He came home with a knot the size of a golf ball on the side of his head, he's limping, and he won't tell me anything. For the last three months he's come home with bruises and cuts and black eyes, and he won't say a thing."

I wondered what it was like to have a mom. She was pissed, all right, but I could see in her expression that she was worried, too. "Is he okay?"

"Brett, please. He won't talk to me. He won't say anything. Ever." She crossed her arms under her breasts, squeezing herself. "What's going on?"

"I don't know, Mrs. Underwood. Can I see him?"

"I'm sorry. He explicitly told me that he didn't want to see you." Her lips tightened, and she narrowed her eyes. "Did you do that to him? Did you hit him?"

"No. A guy at school did." The last thing I wanted was to get into this. Rule number one when your friends' parents grilled you was to find a way to get off the grill. "It's okay, though. They're not after him or anything. I swear. Just a fight."

She narrowed her eyes. "They?"

Ugh. Why did I have to screw everything up? "No, I mean him. The guy. I promise."

Just then, the last person I ever thought would save my life walked into the lobby. Tom. Good old Mr. Boyfriend. He had his hair all done up and gelled like a guy twenty years younger, complete with Ray-Ban sunglasses resting on top. He was dressed in a Hangman Valley Golf Club polo shirt and wore a pair of tan pants. The glasses alone probably cost three hundred bucks, but it didn't change the fact that he was a two-bit ambulance chaser with a loud mouth. He looked at me and grinned. "Hey! Stick! How's the arm?" he said, slapping me on the shoulder like we'd known each other longer than ten minutes.

"Just fine, sir."

He winked knowingly. "I put two thousand on the team. Thanks for the heads-up, kid."

I nodded, smiling inside. "Great," I said, then turned to Preston's mom. "Is he okay?" I asked again.

Tom frowned, but it wasn't a frown of concern. Every second I knew the guy convinced me that God occasionally borrowed from the defective-parts bin when he made people. "Let me guess. Preston."

Preston's mom swallowed. "Tom, tonight isn't a good night. Preston isn't doing well."

"I hope this is some kind of joke, because everybody who's somebody in this city is going to be at this fund-raiser, Diane. It's important."

"Preston was beaten up today at school, Tom."

He grimaced. "Always him. Always the kid. I said this was important."

Word hadn't reached the papers that the star receiver had quit the star team, and I cleared my throat. "Mrs. Underwood? I'm sorry, but I should leave." I glanced at Tom, who still pouted, and I gave him my best smile. "You going to be at the game this week?"

"Yeah, of course. Like I said, I'm betting big on you."

I nodded knowingly. "We're playing Mead. I heard something, too."

He perked up. "Oh yeah?"

"Yeah. Their quarterback messed up his rotator cuff waterskiing yesterday after school. He can't throw."

Tom, with the smell of easy money lingering in his head like a noxious green cloud, clapped his hands. "Golden! I'll up it another thousand." He slapped my back. "Game on, Stick. You're making me money, boy, and this is how it's played!"

I thought about Preston sitting upstairs, no doubt with a raging headache, and I laughed. "You got it, sir."

22

You never do anything dangerous, do you?

Those words rattled around in my head like numbers in a bingo cage. Yeah, right, I thought as my stomach clenched and adrenaline flushed through me. I figured for whatever I hadn't done for the last eighteen years, this was making up for it. Even through my fear, a certain giddiness overcame me, an exhilaration I hadn't felt before.

This was crazy.

After leaving Preston's mom and her boyfriend arguing in the lobby, I sat in the parking lot, staring at the gigantic building. Fifteen minutes later, I watched as Mrs. Underwood's pristine BMW drove from the garage. Tom had won the battle, it looked like. I figured he always got his way, but I also imagined him sitting in the bleachers as the team streamed onto the field this Friday. The look of concern. Then confusion. Then anger when he didn't see me. Then rage when he saw Mead's first-string quarterback take the field. I giggled like a little girl thinking about it.

Now, a half hour later, with the evening breeze rippling through my hair, I looked down. All the way down. On my hands and knees, I peered over the edge of the roof of Preston's building and vertigo swept through me. My eyes swam. I hated heights.

Closing my eyes, I backed away and stood, looking over the twinkling lights of Spokane. A notch of the moon was cresting Brown's Mountain to the east, rising slowly. I could hear the rush of the falls far below, and my eyes were drawn to the headlights, small and distant, streaming along the freeway.

Once again I got on my hands and knees and crept to the spot right above the balcony that was outside Preston's room. Insane. I was insane. I could have buzzed his place after his mom and Tom left, but I didn't. I'd entered the password for the garage and taken the massive lift up to the top floor.

I didn't knock on the door that led into the apartment. Instead, I found the maintenance door and the stairs that led to the roof.

You never do anything dangerous, do you?

The world below me spun, and I laughed. *Trust it.* Trust what was right. I had no idea why I was doing this, but there was a reason, and I was sure it was the right reason.

Among the antennas, air-conditioning units, and other apparatus on the roof, there was a large satellite dish on the south side. Around it, and running along the edge of the roof, were steel bars and tubes that fastened the dish to the building. Fifteen feet below that, Preston's balcony laughed at me. *I dare you to do it.*

I figured that if I slung myself over the edge while gripping the bars, I could dangle a good eight feet down. That left seven feet of flight—or vertical plummet—to his balcony. Every synapse in my body screamed at me to leave. To go knock on his door like a normal human being. Stick Patterson didn't do *anything* that risked his career as a football player. *You never do anything dangerous, do you?* No, I thought. I never do.

I do what I'm told, and I do it without thinking.

No snowboarding, no waterskiing, no dirt bike riding, no diving off the bridge at Post Falls. My dad had actually compiled a list of things I couldn't do. Yellowed with years, it was still posted on the refrigerator. Last year, he'd even nixed plans I had to go play Frisbee golf with my friends the day before a game.

He hadn't, however, written that I couldn't hang over the edge of a nineteen-story building and free-fall to a balcony. Nope. Not on the list. He'd missed that one.

Taking a deep breath, I grasped the bar and twisted sideways, putting my first leg down over the edge. There was no reason to do this. I could have buzzed him. I could have knocked. I could have gone home to face my dad. Preston wasn't in danger. I could talk to him tomorrow. Hunt him down, if need be. But something inside of me said that I had to do this. That he *needed* it. That he needed me to prove something I didn't quite understand. Or maybe that I needed this.

My whole body tight with fear, my heart pounding, I

refused to look at anything but the balcony. As I slung my other leg over the bar, every muscle screamed, and my eyes shifted sideways, to the sparkling lights of the city. *You stupid idiot. Now you've done it.*

Feet dangling, I lowered myself, trying to pretend I was hanging from a monkey bar and not a pipe on the top of a building. Despite the breeze, beads of sweat gathered on my forehead. My body was plastered against the side of the building, my hands white-knuckled on the bar above me. I looked down to the balcony. I had guessed fifteen feet from up there, but here the gap from my toes to the concrete balcony seemed like a hundred.

So I hung there. I could try to pull myself up, but there was nothing farther back on the roof to grab that would allow me to pull myself over to safety. The movies, I realized, were full of crap. There was no way I could swing my leg back up over the bar. I imagined a news helicopter hovering, the camera rolling as they reported on the poor demented teenager hanging over the edge of a nineteen-story building. Breaking News. Eat your dessert and watch the drama unfold.

I don't know how long I hung there, but my hands began to cramp and my shoulder sockets were tortured balls of fire. I was never good at making decisions. Decisions were made for me, and I followed them. Now I was alone. And in a bit of an uncomfortable position.

I looked down again, cussing myself. Count to three and do it. Let go. Tuck and roll just like Vin Diesel or Tom Cruise.

I let go.

I quickly found that tucking and rolling when falling vertically does not work, and the pain that blasted through my body was proof of it. Forward motion was needed to roll. I landed like a collapsing scarecrow, my knees buckling, hitting my chin, my butt slamming into the concrete. I tasted blood, rolled onto my back, and lay there, looking at the faded stars rimming my eyes.

After a minute or so, I detected no broken bones or extreme pain. Just the pain of stupidity, and a crunched tongue. I turned my head and spat a glob of blood and saliva.

Preston didn't have the blinds drawn, and as I lay there, looking into his room, I had a hard time focusing. I'd crashed pretty hard and was surprised I hadn't alerted him.

Taking another breath, I squeezed my eyes shut, then opened them again. The lights were off, and the only glow came from the lamp on his desk. I saw movement through the sliding glass door.

Preston, with shadows drawn about him, stood next to his bed, his clothes bulky. He stuffed items into his school backpack, intent. I shouldn't say stuffed. Preston would never stuff anything anywhere. Whatever he was putting into the pack was carefully placed. Through the dimness, I could only see that what other items he put inside, he did with his typical organized manner.

He was leaving. I was stuck on his balcony. Sudden unease spread through me as I watched him. I was spying, and it didn't feel good. My imagined daring and heroic appearance disappeared, and I was left with being a Peeping Tom.

Groaning, I tore my eyes from him and stared at the star-glittered sky. He was leaving. Where? Why? Had today pushed him over the edge?

As I sat up, my head swam. Before I knew it, Preston had

zipped up the bag and exited his room. Fear gripped me. I rose to my knees and crawled to the door. Please, God, be unlocked. I imagined myself stuck on the balcony all night, the sun rising, Preston's mom coming in and seeing me curled up outside like a homeless stalker freak. Oh God.

Gathering my courage, I crept to the slider. I reached up and pulled on the handle. It slid open gracefully, and I let out a breath. Now that I'd officially gone from a freako stalker to a criminal by breaking and entering, I somehow felt better.

As an attorney, Tom wouldn't agree, I was sure.

I quietly shut the balcony door behind me, then opened the bedroom door. I was just in time to hear the front door shut: Preston leaving. Walking quickly, I decided to leave by way of the kitchen. Once out on the landing, I pressed the elevator button.

In another minute or two, I was breathing the fresh night air outside the car lift, my crimes and humiliation averted.

Then I saw him.

The streetlamps cast his small frame in long shadows as he walked toward the bridge. I had my keys in my hand, and I looked at my car in the distance, then back at his fading figure. I followed, hustling after him.

Across the bridge and to the downtown core, Preston walked quickly, head down, hands in his pockets, hood pulled over his head. Twenty minutes later, he left the business district, turned right, and headed into a neighborhood I'd never been in before.

Nestled against the river, the decrepit houses, broken-down cars, garbage-strewn yards, and barking dogs were more numerous than the occasional well-kept and tidy home. Spokane might not be a sprawling metropolis with all of the metropolitan problems that bigger cities had, but we did have one thing in common with them: not a lot of money.

Hardened people were made hard by scratching a living from low-paying jobs, and more than a few of the neighborhoods showed the wear and tear of an economy that had sputtered and stalled for years. This was one of them.

This late, most houses simply had a porch light burning; some had nothing at all, just black shapes in the night. Streetlights were few and far between, and I had a hard time following Preston. I did notice that he slowed his walk, taking his hands out of his pockets. He turned his head left and right as he went, as if he was looking for an address, and his posture changed, too. His sloped shoulders were squared, his walk steadier.

A car came from behind, its headlights glowing as it drove slowly toward us. I was half a block behind Preston, and as the car passed me, he suddenly stopped and turned around, watching the car come. I stepped behind a massive maple tree next to the sidewalk, watching. The car sped up and drove by, under the pressure of Preston's attention, and as it rounded a corner, Preston broke into a jog, following it.

I, in turn, followed, pacing him, slowing as he rounded the corner. Two blocks up, I saw the taillights of the car disappear once again.

Preston kept jogging, then abruptly stopped. I realized the car hadn't turned a corner. They'd turned their headlights off and were driving slowly toward a car parked on the side of the street.

I couldn't help but wonder what Preston was doing. A drug deal? Trafficking in stolen stuff? Meeting with an assassin to kill Tom, who I was sure had given him the black eye?

I didn't know. Couldn't know with him. Preston was a mystery at every turn. I watched him carefully as I crept closer.

As I did, I saw that the car had stopped. The doors opened. Three figures got out and walked toward the parked car. My skin tingled. Eyes back on Preston. It looked like he was taking his clothes off. I blinked, confused, and the next thing I knew, he was running.

Straight toward the car.

From half a block away, he ran right at them, angling across the street at a sprint. I caught a flash of silver glinting on him as he did. I saw a flowing shadow waving behind him, and as he passed one of the few streetlamps, I gaped.

Preston wasn't Preston. Black tights with silver lightning bolts staggered from hip to ankle. A silver cape edged with jagged black streamed behind him. A black plastic motorcycle chest plate, ribbed with the same silver lightning bolts. Elbow protectors. A utility belt. Black leather gloves. And last but not least, a silver mask covering his eyes.

A superhero.

Preston Underwood thought he was a superhero.

In any other place or time, I would have started laughing uncontrollably. Watching him sprint awkwardly down the street, his knobby knees knocking, his arms pumping, his cape waving, I would have thought it the funniest thing in the world.

But not here. Not now. Not when the full realization of what he was doing slammed into me as hard as the football my dad had drilled into my chest.

You never do anything dangerous, do you?

My breath left me just as I heard the muffled sound of the men breaking the car window. Preston kept on, running closer to them. Intent on breaking into the car, the three men hadn't noticed him charging. I swallowed back a scream, watching in horror as he reached his targets.

He stopped, and just like in every movie I'd ever seen, he faced them, hands on hips. I couldn't hear what he was saying. I did, however, hear them laugh.

They walked toward him.

Just as the first man shoved Preston, I ran. I ran harder and faster than I ever had on the field. Faster than with any football tucked in my arm heading toward a championship. I ran with my teeth clenched, fear in my heart, tears gathering in my eyes, and panic coursing through every fiber of my body.

When Preston slammed into the ground, I lowered my shoulder and hit the first guy harder than Tilly had ever pounded an offensive lineman into the turf. I *felt* the air leave him, heard his teeth crunch together, saw his feet leave the ground, and heard his ribs snapping.

The guy flew backwards, then skidded across the pavement. My momentum carried me on top of him. His head snapped back and hit the pavement, and he went out like a light. I stared into his slack face, wondering for an instant if I'd killed him. Then I heard a scream.

It wasn't Preston. I twisted, turning to look back, and

there was Preston, sitting on his butt, calmly spraying a canister of pepper spray into the face of the second man. The guy sprang away, writhing, clawing at his burning eyes, screaming bloody murder as he inhaled the fire.

With the canister empty and the third guy coming at him, Preston scrambled at his belt, fumbling for something.

"Stop!" I heard the word coming from my throat, a bellow more than a scream, before I knew I said it. The man did stop. He looked at me. He was big. Bigger than me. Around twenty or so, he had a scraggly goatee and wore a Harley Davidson shirt, and his eyes were dark discs in the shadows cast by the streetlight. He glanced at his buddies, one still writhing on the ground, slobbering pepper spray and mucus, the other laid out cold on the concrete.

Anger replaced my fear, and just like the lightning bolts running down Preston's costume, it struck me. I stomped toward him, fists balled, ready to take the beating Preston had taken for me.

The guy blinked, looking from me to Preston, who sat calmly, staring at me. The man shook his head. "You're crazy." Then he ran.

The pepper-sprayed man groveled on the ground, rubbing his eyes. Preston frowned at me. "What are you doing here, Brett?"

I walked over to him, reaching down and offering my hand in the semi-darkness. The stars still glimmered, the rage faded, the street was quiet, and I looked into his masked eyes. "I guess I'm helping a . . . superhero."

23

"You're not Batman."

He'd put his pants and hoodie back on, and I almost felt like what had just happened was normal. He adjusted the backpack on his shoulder. "Batman isn't real, Brett."

I stopped, remembering the black eye, the bruises. Those guys would have torn him apart tonight. Then again, when I'd turned back to him after the guy ran away, he'd had a Taser in his hands. "Preston, this isn't a joke. You're not a superhero."

When he'd gotten back into his regular clothes, his usual demeanor returned. Slump-shouldered, hands in his pockets, and passive, he looked at me. "You are, though."

"What?"

His eyes pierced mine. "You dress up in a colorful costume and pretend you're something you're not every Friday night to play a game. I do the same thing, but there are two differences between us."

"What?"

"The first is that when *you* dress up like an idiot and beat the crap out of your opponents, thousands of people think you're sane. They cheer and they clap and they wish they were you."

"And the second?"

His expression hardened, and his voice was like a viper's hiss. "The second? The second difference is that what you do is completely useless. It's idiotic. You play a game for points on a scoreboard. There's no value to it, and therefore, there's no value to you."

"This is your way of thanking me?" I pointed back the way we came. "I might play a stupid game, but I don't go out risking my life for a stolen stereo! You're the idiot, Preston."

He spoke quickly, anger and contempt lacing his voice. "I wasn't thanking you, and perhaps you didn't know it, but there are two million high school sports injuries a year in this country, thirteen point two percent of which are head injuries. Anybody with an ounce of logic would realize that suffering a head injury for no reason is the definition of being an idiot, but I didn't call you an idiot. I called football idiotic, which is different, but you wouldn't know that because your brain can't handle anything more complicated than how many steps to run in a pattern so you can catch a ball."

"Well, that doesn't matter anymore because I quit— remember? And besides, even if football is useless, what you're doing is useless, too."

He swung his backpack at me full-force, and in the next second he was on me, flapping his arms, slapping me, trying to hit me. I felt like I was being attacked by a herd of sixth-grade girls. Hunching over and putting my arms over my head, I waited until he was finished.

Finally he stood back, panting, his eyes wild, staring at me.

I peeked at him through the crook of my elbow, expecting another flurry. "Are you done?"

He kicked his backpack, sending it into the street. "I know I'm not a superhero! I know I'm not strong or tough and I can hardly walk down the street without tripping over my own fucking feet, but if I'd just been able to do something when—" He stopped suddenly, swallowing, and I saw tears in his eyes.

In the next breath, he snatched up his pack and ran. His footsteps echoed down the street as he disappeared into the darkness. And as I watched him go, I knew I'd hurt him. This *wasn't* a game to him, and it wasn't pretending. I felt like a fool. There was nothing for him to win, I realized, because he couldn't win his father back to life.

24

I cut the headlights and coasted to the curb in front of my house. Thank God there were no lights on, and as I opened the car door, I hoped my dad was beer-sleeping. A tornado wouldn't wake the guy up when he fell asleep with a beer in his hand.

I knew I was in all kinds of trouble. I'd stolen back my car, which he knew about now for sure; I'd quit the team and declined a scholarship; and at one-thirty in the morning I was way past my curfew. A week ago if I'd ever thought of doing those things, I'd have thought I'd be better off slitting my wrists and jumping off a bridge.

As I tiptoed up the porch stairs, I grunted. Tiptoeing? It was like sneaking back into prison. Straightening, I opened the front door. It banged into something. Pushing, I moved whatever it was and poked my head in, looking down.

There, barely glinting from the moonlight, was a box full

of every trophy I'd ever won. I smiled. At least it was a big box.

"Those are yours."

His voice came from the recliner. His words were slurred, but not like the usual drunk-and-half-asleep slur. I stepped inside. He turned the lamp on.

I shut the door. "I'm sorry I'm late and I'm sorry I took my car. I should have told you."

He pointed to the box. "You earned those. Keep them. Nothing else, though." He held his hand out. "Keys."

I looked down at the box, then back at him. "What's going on?"

"It means you no longer live here. You take your trophies and get out."

"Dad, come on. I said I wa—"

"GET OUT!" he boomed.

He was half drunk, but this wasn't just the booze talking. The football drilling my chest flashed through my mind. I wondered for a second if he'd turned into a total jerk or if I'd just gotten old enough to know he'd always been one. "Okay. I'll pack my clothes and leave."

He shook his head. "You take the clothes on your back and that box full of wasted dreams. Get out."

"Dad, come on."

"You screwed up, Brett. You've thrown away everything you've been given, and this is what happens to people like that. Give me the keys."

"No."

He stood, his eyes boring into me. "Now!"

"Or what? You got a football you want to hit me with?

Maybe grab me and shake me? That's one of your favorites, right? Throw me up against the wall? Slap me again?" I stared right back at him. "You know what I did tonight? I tried to help a kid who lost his dad. Murdered right in front of him. He goes out and tries to make the world a better place because of it. You know what I do? I catch a fucking ball. That's all I'm supposed to do, right? And now your poor little world is ruined."

He came at me, his eyes flaring, and as he did, I raised my hands and shoved him. Hard. He flew back, crashing against the recliner and falling to the floor. His expression showed that he was as stunned as I was. I swallowed, then shook my head. "You're never going to touch me again. All I wanted was a dad. Just a dad. Not a coach or mentor or teacher. Just a dad." I looked at the box of trophies, then kicked. They flew across the room, scattering. "I'm keeping my keys," I said.

He blinked, staring.

I slammed the door shut on the way out.

25

Back in my car, I drove to the nearest parking lot and sat. Then I dialed Mike. I got his message, then called again. He answered on the fifth ring. "Hey, Brett," he said, his voice sleepy.

"Hey," I said, uncomfortable. "What's up?"

"Well, it's two a.m. I was sleeping."

"Yeah. Sorry. You mind if I camp out at your house tonight? My dad and I got into it."

He hesitated. "I heard about today with Tilly and Killinger. Your new friend went apeshit on them."

"If that's what they say."

"He's the one with the eggs, right?"

"Yeah."

"Both of them are gunning for you now. You know that, right?" he said.

"It doesn't matter anymore. I'm done."

"You're not coming back to the team?"

"No."

He paused again. "I can't believe you're doing this, Brett."

"You know why I am, Mike. And I figured you'd get it."

"That's funny."

"What is?" I said.

"For the first time, I agree with your dad and Coach more than you."

Our friendship flashed through my head. Years of backyard campouts. Playing ball in the street. Riding our bikes down to the pond and chasing ducks. Joining Boy Scouts and quitting at the same time. Checking out girls downtown. "Don't do this, Mike."

"Do what? Be pissed that you're fucking everybody over, including your best friend?"

"If the only thing I am to you is a way to get something you want, I guess so."

"Killinger was right."

"Right about what?"

"He said you couldn't cut it. That this is how they cull the weak from the strong."

"So I guess this is it, then? All this for nothing."

Mike didn't answer, and the silence was deafening.

"You're better than them, Mike. You are," I said. Then I hung up.

26

I woke up at six with a stiff neck, a cramp in my foot, and a headache. Newly homeless, I'd curled up in the back of my car, spreading an old hoodie over me and hoping that bandits, car thieves, murderers, or traveling gypsies wouldn't kill me.

Sitting up, I watched the sun brighten the sky and took stock of what I had. Fourteen dollars and seven cents in my pockets. Fifty-three dollars in the bank. A half-dead cell phone with no charger. A quarter tank of gas. The clothes I had on my back. A new freedom that I found oddly exhilarating.

I'd finally stood up to my dad, and I'd seen the look in his eyes. He'd believed me. He'd known I was serious. *He'd listened.* He would never touch me again. He'd never make me live the way he wanted me to live, and sitting in my garbage-strewn car, I knew that I preferred this to that. Things were different now, and even though I was freaked out about what the heck to do, I knew I'd do something.

I also knew I wasn't going back home.

That struck me almost like a blow. Everything with my dad had always been a lesson. A teaching moment, he said. Punishment was a learning experience. This wasn't. He couldn't punish me any longer. He'd expected me to act like a man since I was twelve years old, and now that I was making my own decisions, he couldn't accept that.

I wondered for the millionth time what it would be like if my mom was alive, but I put it out of my head. I used to fantasize when I was little, usually after I'd gotten in trouble. My mom was always the hero. The superhero, I thought, then laughed, thinking of Preston. She would always rescue me in my fantasies. Hug me. Tell me everything was okay, and that I was okay.

I knew different, though. If she was alive, she'd be gone. Away from him. And maybe, just maybe, I'd be with her, living a different life.

Pulling myself out of my own mud hole, I thought about the positives. I had wheels and I had the clothes on my back, even if they were wrinkled and crumpled. I also had an empty belly. Deciding that the breakfast of champions would be a 7-Eleven breakfast burrito, I picked the one that didn't look eight years old, grabbed a Gatorade, and ate in my car.

Fifteen minutes later, and with a lump of lead in my stomach, I had to decide about school. The last thing I wanted to do was go, but something inside of me, a new thing, told me I needed to. Not to learn, but to at least not give in. If I was honest with myself, Lance Killinger scared me. Tilly might have the muscles, but Lance was far more dangerous because he knew how to play more than football.

27

"I don't know what to do."

Mr. Reeves looked at me, contemplating. He tapped his pen on his desk. "About what, Brett? Football?"

"No. Well, yes. Everything has just sort of fallen apart."

He nodded, but didn't say anything. We'd been talking for ten minutes and getting nowhere. He wasn't the type to press, and I wasn't the type to tell people the truth about how I felt about things.

I went on. "If I tell you stuff, is it private?"

"Yes."

I knew he was full of crap because I'd Googled confidentiality with school counselors on my phone that morning. If he thought I was in danger—a danger to myself or being abused—he *had* to report it to the authorities. After reading that, I'd laughed. It meant anybody with any serious problems might as well sew their mouth shut rather than talk to a counselor with any honesty.

But I had to trust him, because on my way to school I realized that I truly didn't know what to do. I was more lost than I'd ever been. So I told him. Everything. Football, my dad, Coach watching the fight, Tilly, Killinger, and last but not least, Preston. I didn't tell Mr. Reeves his name, though. The last thing I wanted was Preston sitting in the hot seat because I'd blabbed.

And when I finished telling him, he looked at me, and my world crumbled. So much for trust.

Mr. Reeves took a breath. "You are being harassed, physically assaulted, and bullied by fellow students. They could be suspended and put into mandatory counseling. Your father, by throwing the football at you, could be charged with domestic violence or child abuse. He could also possibly be charged with neglect for kicking you out of the house with no means to support yourself. Coach Williams could be severely disciplined for allowing students to fight. Your friend, whoever he is, puts himself in life-threatening situations and is in need of immediate counseling." He stopped and stared at me.

"What are you going to do?"

He shook his head. "No, Brett. That's not what this is about. *You're* going to tell *me* what to do."

"But that *is* what this is about. I don't know what to do."

He shook his head again. "I misled you when I said this conversation was private. I had no idea the severity of the situation. I assumed you were dealing with the typical problems surrounding quitting a team." He paused. "But that doesn't mean I need to force things all at once. I'm a counselor, and under those same laws, I have leeway."

"Then what? What are you going to do? My dad might be an asshole, but he shouldn't be arrested."

He nodded. "First, I clear my afternoon. Second, I excuse you from your classes. Then you figure out what you need to do while I sit here and listen."

28

"Nice window," Preston said. He'd been standing by my car after school, waiting.

I looked at the empty space where my rear window had been. "Thanks."

He shuffled. "It would complicate my life if you told my mom what I do."

"Is that why you were waiting here? To tell me that?"

"Partially."

I stepped to the rear of my car. "One of the good things about having a convertible," I said as I threw my pack into the backseat, "is ease of use."

He watched me as I unlocked the door, then pointedly looked at the gaping hole in the back of my car. "Are you afraid somebody will steal something from the front?"

I looked down at the key in the lock and laughed. "You need a lift home?"

He shook his head. "I said I was partially waiting for you to ask you not to tell my mom about me."

"What's the other part?"

"I told you that football was useless."

"It is."

He shook his head. "But I think you're making a mistake by quitting."

"I hate playing, Preston. And besides, you basically told me to quit, so why are you telling me not to now?"

"You hate all the reasons you give yourself to play. Your dad, the assholes you play with, that gorilla they call the coach. They're all controlling you. That's what I was telling you, Brett."

I realized he was the only person I knew who had never called me Stick. "No. I quit. I have the power, Preston. I finally stood up for myself. Don't you get that? You of all people should."

"When you quit, you gave *them* all the power. I've seen you play, and even though I think it's a stupid waste of time and played by below-average human beings, you're good at what you waste your time doing. Really good."

"You have a horrible way of complimenting people."

He leaned against my car. "Be honest. You love playing football, don't you?"

"Of course I do. But it's all just . . ."

"It's all just too much for you to take? You're good at pretending to be stupid, Brett, but it gets tiring after a while," he said. "You *let* them ruin what you love. Admit that, at least."

I bit my lip and watched as the few remaining cars in the parking lot filtered out. "There's no other way to do it, though. All the strings are attached. And besides, after Coach watching you get beat up, I would never play for him." I spat. "Jesus, even if I was willing to go back, Lance and Tilly would make my life hell." I shook my head angrily, glancing at him. "Listen, Preston, I know I screwed up. The day I quit, I knew. But I quit for the right reasons. Football—or anything else for that matter—shouldn't be this way."

He stood there with his fingers in his pockets, feet splayed like a duck, shoulders slumped, a skinny rail of a kid with an enormous amount of wisdom that I couldn't fathom. "My dad shouldn't be dead, either. Nothing is ever the way it should be."

"So that's why you thwart crime in a costume."

He shook his head. "The costume doesn't do anything important, Brett, just like your costume doesn't do anything. After my dad died, everybody said I should deal with it the way everybody else does. But that didn't work." He paused, shifting on his feet. "I tried to jump off that bridge." He looked at me. "But I couldn't. That's why I go back and walk the ledge. To remind myself."

I'd originally thought he was just a weird and sad dork pretending to be Batman. Some overgrown six-year-old with no friends who still played with action figures. "I guess I don't have to do things the way they say, huh?"

"I'm the one with the mental problems. You're the star."

I laughed. "I think you're the most sane person I've ever met. Weird, but sane." Somehow, I felt better, but it didn't leave me with any answers. "I can't go back to the team, though. I won't."

He smiled. "You are really stupid sometimes."

"What now?"

He hitched his pack on his shoulders. "I heard the Tigers are tied for first with the Saxons, since you guys lost last week. I also know that there are emergency school transfer policies for students who are being bullied."

I blinked, widening my eyes.

"Walk the ledge, Brett. Your way—not the way you're supposed to," he said.

I bolted back to Mr. Reeves's office.

29

I knocked until he answered. He'd changed the locks. I could tell by the haze in his eyes he'd downed a few beers, and he scowled when he saw me. "I told you . . ."

I held out a sheet of paper and a pen to him. "I need your signature."

He looked at the paper with the Hamilton Saxon standard emblazoned on the top. He brightened. "You decided to play, then? Coach said if you decided to rejoin, I'd need to sign another release form."

"I'm playing."

He grinned. "I knew you'd come around, son. Come in, come in. I had a spare key made. I'll get it for you." He clapped me on the back and went inside.

I followed, the paper still in my hand. He sat down, and I gave it to him. He was shaking his head and smiling as he signed. "Sometimes it takes tough love to show you where you should be, Brett. I always had faith in you. Always. And we can put last night out of our heads. I set your trophies back up."

I took the paper from him, folding it. A sudden jab of guilt hit me. I knew he'd sign the transfer without reading it. I also knew he loved me, but maybe not the right way. "I've got to get this down to Lewis and Clark before five. Coach Larson said he'd wait."

"What? Larson? Lewis and Clark?" he said.

"Yeah."

He looked at the sheet in my hands. "Hold on here, Brett. I thought we—"

I *was* playing football again, and I was playing it on my own terms. If my dad couldn't accept that, it was his issue to deal with. "I know. I'm excited, too. They're a good team, and Coach Larson said if I show myself during practice this week and next, I can start wide receiver a week from Friday. It's against Shadle."

His face went dark. He'd gone to Hamilton as a teenager. He'd played Hamilton ball with Coach Williams. He jabbed a finger at the paper. "What did I just sign?"

"Transfer slip. Mr. Reeves said I could have an emergency transfer because the team is bullying me. I'm playing for Lewis and Clark, Dad," I said, then bent and picked up the extra door key. "Thanks for this, too. I don't know how late I'll be. I have to start studying the playbook and watching their tapes."

He gawked as I left. I could almost feel the silent explosions going off in his head.

30

Coach Larson shook my hand and ushered me into his office. I'd never met him before, but the slender, youngish-looking man seemed nice enough. A picture of a woman and three kids, younger than me, stood on his desk.

He was all teeth through his smiles, but there was an undercurrent in the tone of his voice, and I couldn't tell if he was happy to meet Brett Patterson or happy to have the best receiver in the state on his team. I hoped both. He took a seat, gesturing to one of the chairs in front of his desk. "This is a surprise, son."

"To me, too, sir."

He took his baseball cap off and scratched his head. "I've been thinking on how to do this ever since your counselor called me this afternoon, and I can't say I'm too comfortable with the situation."

"How is that, Coach?"

"It's going to look like I . . . ," he began, then stopped. "You're transferring due to some bullying that went on. I'm assuming it was because you quit the team."

"Yessir."

He adjusted his cap. "Then let's get one thing straight. It ends here. I coach fair and I fight hard. My team does, too. I'm sure Coach Williams will change his playbook after hearing about this, but if I hear one word out of your mouth that gives the Tigers an unfair advantage on the field, you're benched for the season." His eyes bore into mine, his smile gone. "You understand that, son? I play fair."

I laughed, full of relief.

"You find what I just said funny, Brett?"

"No, sir. Not at all. I just wasn't expecting . . . I just want to play football. Fair football."

He extended his hand across the desk. We shook, hard and strong. "Then welcome to my team." He tossed a play-book to me. "Practice at five-thirty tomorrow morning. You study up. Just because you've got all those numbers stacked up around you doesn't mean you walk onto my team. You don't prove it, you don't play. Earn it, Brett. Now get out of my office."

On my way home, I was almost giddy with excitement. I would play, and I would play my way. The right way. And in the process, I'd watch Coach Williams and Lance Killinger wish they never knew me.

31

I couldn't sleep. I usually hit my bed and was out like a light, but my mind ran circles thinking about what would happen. Preston telling me I was Superman jabbed through my thoughts, and finally I gave up on sleep and grabbed my phone.

He answered on the second ring. "Hey."

"Hey."

"You up?"

"Unless you're having a particularly lucid dream, yes, I'm up," Preston said.

I glanced at the clock. A few minutes before twelve. "What are you doing?"

"Why are you calling, Brett?"

"I transferred to the Tigers."

"And you wanted to chat about it at midnight?"

"I couldn't sleep. Are you out?"

"Out what?"

"Doing your thing. You know. Crime-fighting stuff."

"Yes, I am."

Fifteen minutes later, I pulled up to the corner of Sixth and Fiske. Preston hopped in. "Any luck?"

Tonight he was in full regalia. No hoodie, no sweats covering his costume. "I wouldn't consider people being victimized by crime as lucky, but no. Most times I go out, I don't see anything."

"Don't you feel weird walking around like that?"

"No."

I drove. "Where do you want to go?"

"Stay around this area. This neighborhood has the highest crime statistics in the city."

"How do you know this stuff?"

"The police department has a detailed crime map online. And I keep my own records. Serial robberies generally follow a pattern. You just have to figure it out." He pointed to a small convenience store up the block. "They've been robbed three times in the last six months."

"What's the pattern there?"

"The only thing I could figure is that it's happened every other month, on the night of the fifteenth, and between twelve-thirty and one-thirty."

"Why?"

"Payday is on the fifteenth. Stores like that sell cigarettes and beer like crazy on paydays. They have a lot of cash in the till."

I blinked. "And today is . . ."

"The fifteenth," he said. "And they weren't robbed last month. If there is a pattern, it'll happen in the next forty-five minutes."

A chill ran through me. "That's pretty cool. Almost like one of those FBI profiler guys."

"Pull over up there. In front of that blue truck."

I did. "The first time I ever saw a crime happen was with you. Those guys and the car."

"That's because you don't look for it. And besides, if you research the right areas, your odds of seeing something go up dramatically. Turn the engine off."

"I've seen cashiers at 7-Eleven put cash in tubes and drop them in a safe. Why don't these guys do that?"

"Manuel Cruz. He's from Venezuela. He opened up the store himself when he immigrated here. It's not corporate. Just a mom-and-pop place. They live in the apartment upstairs. Two kids, nine and eleven."

"What *don't* you know, Preston?"

He shrugged. "It's all public record."

We sat in the dark, the silence comfortable as we watched the late-night traffic go in and out of the store. Preston wasn't one for small talk, and after a few minutes, he buried his nose in his phone.

"Bored?" I said.

He kept his eyes on the phone. "No. A man in a blue Accord just parked on the side street across from the place. I'm looking up his license plate."

"Why?"

"Because he's sitting there doing what we're doing, and

there are only two reasons for that. I somehow don't think stopping crime is on his mind."

"Maybe he's just stopping to get something."

"Across the street? When the parking lot is nearly empty?" he said, tapping his phone. "Connor Tatum. Thirty-one years old. Convicted of shoplifting, theft, grand larceny, and strong-arm robbery. Get ready."

"You're sure?"

"No."

A thrill went through me as I watched the car. I felt like I was on some sort of reality show like *Cops*, just with a hundred-and-seventeen-pound kid dressed in a costume instead of fully trained officers who knew what they were doing. "So what do we do?"

Just as he put his mask on, the Accord's door opened and a man got out. "We see what happens."

My heart raced as the man pulled his hood over his head and strode across the parking lot to the front door. "No, I mean, do we go in now? Stop it?"

"We wait until it's over, then detain him. Statistically, interrupting a crime like this in progress endangers the victim more than the crime itself does."

The man reached the building and went inside. We watched as he spoke to the cashier. Then all hell broke loose.

Just as the man took his hand from his pocket, the cashier literally *launched* himself over the counter, tackling the guy and driving him into a rack of Hostess doughnuts. Blood pounded in my ears and I tightened as the two men went down and out of sight. "Preston . . ."

"Change of plans," he calmly said, dialing 911 and opening

his door. "Yes. Robbery in progress. Fourth and Stevens." He hung up and threw his phone on the seat.

In the next moment I was out of the car, running after Preston. His cape flapped in the night air. As we neared the store, there was the crack of a gunshot, and I slowed, fear stabbing through me. "Preston! NO! He's got a gun!" I screamed.

Preston kept running, and when he flung the door open, this exciting little adventure stopped being anything but terrifyingly real and ugly. This wasn't a game, and the reality that Preston wasn't playacting at being a superhero hit me square in the stomach. He was willing to risk his life for what he believed in. For his guilt. For his father.

Something in me snapped, and I sprinted again. Not to the car, not away, not to my home and my bedroom and my safe life. I ran after my friend. My crazy friend.

I hit the door and saw the blood. Dark and thick, pooling from underneath the body of the cashier. The floor was strewn with doughnuts, candy bars, beer cans, and bags of chips. A stainless steel pistol gleaming in the fluorescent lights caught my eye. The remnants of pepper spray stung my eyes.

Preston was struggling furiously with the robber. They were next to the condiment section, and bottles of mayonnaise, catsup, and mustard were flying everywhere. He'd somehow disarmed the man, and as I jumped to help him, two little girls and a woman, all in nightgowns, rushed from around a corner at the back of the store and began shrieking and screaming at the sight of the cashier lying in a pool of blood.

Preston, now sprawled on top of the guy, and with what looked like catsup and mustard smeared on his face, frantically reached into a pouch on his belt and took out his Taser. "Z-z-zip ties," he stammered, looking at me as he jammed the Taser against the man's exposed belly.

I blinked, not understanding. The man suddenly stiffened, a silent scream frozen on his face.

"Zip ties! GET THE FUCKING ZIP TIES!" Preston screamed, and I was jolted out of my frozen terror.

Yanking at the pair of white plastic zip ties on Preston's belt, I knelt over the still-being-electrocuted guy and grabbed his wrists, sliding the ties over his hands and cinching them tight.

Without a breath, Preston heaved himself from the guy and scrambled through the mess to the cashier. He leaned over the man and ripped open the bloody T-shirt. "Help me. It's through the chest." Blood pumped from the wound in tandem with the heart, spilling his life away. Preston jammed his finger into the hole. "It went all the way through. Reach under his back, find the exit wound, and stuff your finger in it. He's bleeding to death."

I did so, feeling the sticky, slick texture of the blood. I gritted my teeth. I almost retched. "It's big. Bigger than my finger."

"Use two fingers. Just get it plugged."

Sirens howled closer, and as the woman and two girls crowded around, Preston looked at the woman. *"No morira."*

She gazed back at him, then nodded. *"Eres valiente. Gracias,"* she said, then cupped her husband's head in her hands and kissed his brow. *"Gracias."*

• • •

Two hours after the paramedics took Manuel to the hospital and the police had interviewed us, with Preston blithely telling them he'd been at a costume party and happened to be in the store when the shooting occurred, I sat in my bedroom. Picking up my phone, I Googled *"No morira."* It meant "He won't die" in Spanish. Then I looked up *"Eres valiente."*

"You are brave."

32

BRETT PATTERSON, STAR RECEIVER
FOR THE HAMILTON SAXONS,
TRANSFERS TO LEWIS AND CLARK

I read the sports section headline on my phone as I sat in the parking lot before practice. Word traveled fast. There wasn't anything in the news about the shooting last night, and it didn't escape me that a father of two could almost die in an armed robbery and it was ignored, but me switching teams made headlines.

I'd left before my dad woke up, thanking heaven for an early getaway, and as I got out of my car and headed toward the gym, I pushed him as far out of my mind as possible. I was here for one thing: playing ball.

I knew a few guys on the team, but the two I needed to know, I didn't. One was the quarterback, a six-foot-five beanpole named Ben Lynch, who was known for passing long balls better than most. He had a hell of an arm, but he couldn't run worth anything. The other was Jordan Appleway, their star receiver.

Tension filled me as I neared the doors, and I stopped, taking a few breaths.

"Patterson."

I turned, and a guy stood up from a bench by the entrance. Ben Lynch. He smiled, the Adam's apple on his long neck bobbing as he talked. "Coach told me to meet you. Show you around."

We shook hands. Dressed in faded jeans, a flannel shirt, and work boots, he looked like an incredibly tall farm boy. He talked like one, too, drawling his words like a weathered ranch hand. I nodded. "Thanks."

He laughed. "You might as well have set off a nuclear bomb in this town. Shit hit the fan, for sure, and it's just going to get worse."

After what had happened at the convenience store, the meaning of "shit hit the fan" was forever changed, and it didn't include a football game. "Things change, huh?"

He showed me inside. "Whole team knew it by ten last night. You see the news this morning?"

I held up my phone. "Yeah. Sort of stupid, huh?"

He led me down the corridor, laughing. "It might be a game, but people take this crap seriously. You do know that three thousand Saxon fans hate your guts right about now? And that doesn't include every guy in town that went to Hamilton for the last fifty years."

I grinned. "Yeah, pretty well aware of that one."

He opened the door to the locker room and showed me my space. He pointed to the locker. "Suit's inside. And no worries. Coach says you're a Tiger, you're a Tiger. We got your back long as you got ours. Even if you did play for Hamilton."

I wasn't so sure about that. I'd seen my friends turn on me in the course of a weekend, and besides an overriding anger toward Tilly and Killinger, no matter how much I didn't want to admit it, it hurt. Especially Mike. "Thanks," I said, sitting on the bench and unlacing my sneakers.

He paused, then went on. "You got anything to tell me about their defense?"

"Yeah. They play it well."

He grinned wide, then pointed to his face. "Know what this is?"

I shook my head.

"It's a shit-eatin' grin. Test passed. Coach told me to say that. Welcome to the Tigers." He clapped me on the back, then wandered off down the aisle, laughing.

I opened my locker. The orange and black of the Tigers greeted me, and I looked at the shiny new uniform, thinking of Preston. I could do this. If he could walk the ledge, so could I.

As the locker room filled, a few guys came by to introduce themselves. All nice guys, and the locker room was just like usual. Guys jabbing each other, throwing out good-natured insults, talking shit about hot girls. Nobody called me Stick until a black kid, black as midnight and with a swagger to his walk, came up to me. No handshake, no smile, just a neutral stare. He looked me up and down. "My oh my. I bet all the girls love you."

I had no response to that.

"They call you Stick, right?" His voice was high, and his words tumbled out smooth and fast.

"Yeah."

He sat down on the bench, straddling it. "You ain't Stick here."

I laced my cleats. "Okay."

"I know you," he said. "I watch your tapes, read the articles, hear everybody talk. You're good. Better than me."

I straightened from my cleats, turning to him, ready for the usual. First-string wide receiver Jordan Appleway, the guy I was gunning for, didn't seem to be a nice guy. More like an arrogant prick, which reminded me of Lance. "Oh yeah?"

"Yeah, oh yeah. But that doesn't mean diddly. You've got to earn it. Nothing free, and you ain't walking on that field without walking over me first." He stood up, smiling even wider. "You ain't Stick till you earn Stick. I play for this team, not for me. You do the same, you got first spot. Plain and simple, babyface. Play for the team. My team."

I stood up, and he did, too. "Yeah."

He put his hand out. I shook it. Jordan Appleway wasn't the person I thought he would be. And I would—I would play for the team. And I would kick his ass in the process.

He laughed. "You think you got me, babyface. You manage to kick me down, I'm all butt-hurt, right? Naw." He shook his head. "I'll still be first string, just right side." He pointed down the aisle to a brown-haired kid suiting up who was glancing at us uncomfortably. "Dillon Yance, otherwise known as Sponge. He's all we got besides me. He's the one you're going to kick down to second string. Got horseshoes on his feet and clay in his head, but we ain't got nothing else, and he's a good guy."

I smiled. Jordan Appleway was a different person, and I liked it. "Got it."

33

Practice was grueling, as usual, and even though I struggled with new plays and players, I reminded myself why I was doing this. The right way. My way. And any coach who didn't put you on the brink of heart failure getting ready for a game wasn't a coach. Coach Larson was well aware of it, and had no trouble breaking the new guy in.

Though I was awkward and uncomfortable being on the Tigers' field, thoughts of betrayal and retribution disappeared, and I smiled as we drilled through plays. The old feeling was back. I was busting my ass because it was fun.

Thirty minutes into practice, I noticed that the attitude of the Tigers was different. Definitely competitive, the guys slung challenging insults back and forth constantly, but there wasn't an edge to it. Then I realized why. Coach Larson could bellow and rage with the best of them, but he never made it personal. He didn't belittle players like Coach

Williams did, and for every time he raked somebody over the coals for a missed step or bad play, he slapped a back or clapped for a good one. He also laughed.

I didn't know that football coaches were capable of laughing.

While Coach put me through the cycle, Ben Lynch, tall, gangly, and seemingly uncomfortable in his body, was actually much more disciplined than Killinger. Every step was calculated, every throw was timed perfectly, and he had a natural feel for the motion of the game. He wasn't as talented as Killinger, but he made up for it with precision. He was also a nice guy.

Jordan Appleway, on the other hand, called me babyface no less than a dozen times, and trash-talked me up and down, all with a smile. By the sweat on this face and the hustle he gave Coach, he was holding true to his word. He was fighting hard for top position.

I was, too.

At lunch and while searching for my new classes, I found it nice to be mostly anonymous. Lewis and Clark didn't live and breathe football, and I guessed that not even ten percent of the students knew who I was. Just a new kid. It was almost like I'd moved to a different city, really, and it didn't take me long to notice that the whole vibe at LC was different. There were cliques, sure, but they weren't as rigid here. I saw skaters hanging with jocks, punks walking down the halls with drama geeks, and teachers talking casually with students.

I decided I liked it, even though my stomach squirmed whenever I thought of my old team.

By fourth period, I had fourteen texts. By fifth period I had twenty. By the time I left school, thirty-five texts told me I was a traitor, an asshole, a faggot, a turncoat. Two of them, one from Killinger and one from Tilly, said I should watch my back.

Every player on the Hamilton team had texted me, some more than once. Except for one person. Mike. He called me.

I picked up, and he didn't wait a second. "You really did it, huh?" he yelled. "You couldn't just quit. You couldn't just ruin our season, huh? You had to do this? The Tigers? You are the biggest dick in the world, Brett."

I listened, heard the anger and hate in his voice, and took a breath. I realized also that when the Tigers played Hamilton, Mike would be covering me as a defensive end. "I take it we're not friends anymore, then?" I said.

"Friends? You're kidding me, man. Friends don't do this."

"When did football become more important than us, Mike?"

"Listen, Brett, I don't know what we are, but I know you ruined any slight chance I had at playing college ball. You get that—right? I know I'm not good enough to go pro, but scouts were noticing us, and if we had bagged another championship, I would have had a shot."

How many nights had we sat talking about college? About playing together? About scholarships? We'd talk for hours, dreaming about stadiums and crowds, but never this way. "I'm sorry about that, Mike, but I'm not playing ball for any of those reasons now."

"And you call yourself a friend?" he replied, acid on his tongue.

"Yeah, I do. And a good one. But I'm not responsible for you. You are."

"So you dump on me. And the team. Great."

"You do know that Coach Williams watched Tilly and Killinger gang up on Preston?"

"Yeah."

"Yeah," I said. "And I'm not playing for a man like that. He's the kind of coach that ruins this game. And you know what? Even after my first practice this morning, I see that, and I don't know how I was so blind for the last three years about it. I love this game, Mike, and I'm not going to let other people ruin it for me anymore. If you can't understand that, I'm sorry."

His voice softened. "Tilly and Killinger—hell, half the team—are after you now. And it's not just you. Killinger has a major ax to grind with your new little buddy."

"Preston doesn't have anything to do with this, Mike. And besides, you have no idea what he is. Who he is."

"Yeah, well, you tell that to Lance. The kid is open game as far as the team is concerned."

"Including you?" I said.

Silence. "If there's anybody I'd like to beat the crap out of, it's you." He paused, then sighed. "We had state in the bag."

"This isn't about football anymore, Mike, and you know it," I said, then hung up.

34

I called Preston three times after talking with Mike, and a surge of panic rose in me when he didn't answer. I had visions of destruction rolling through my head as I got in my half-convertible car. I'd seen Killinger and Tilly work their magic on unsuspecting nerds and geeks, and I knew full well that they weren't going after Preston to humiliate him.

They were going after him to hurt him.

Tracking Preston down was becoming a habit, and I ground my teeth in frustration as I drove to his place. I buzzed his apartment, and his mom answered.

"Hello, Mrs. Underwood. It's Brett. Is Preston home?"

"Brett, I don't think this is a good time . . . ," she began, and then I heard a male voice in the background tell her to buzz me up. A short conversation, muffled, followed. "Come on up, Brett."

When I reached the top floor, I knocked on the door, and

it swung open so quickly that it startled me. Tom stood there, dressed like a glorified used-car salesman. He smiled, leaning forward, but there was ice in his eyes. "Well, if it isn't Brett Patterson, in person. Come on in!" he said, the tone of his voice like a viper ready to strike.

"Is Preston here?" I said, but it went unanswered as Tom walked back into the apartment, leaving the door open.

I stepped in, quietly closing the door behind me, and Mrs. Underwood came in from the kitchen. She smiled, but the lines around her mouth were tense. "Preston is in his room," she said, nodding pointedly down the hall.

I turned to head down to his room, but Tom's voice boomed from the living room. "Things sure change quickly, eh, Patterson?"

I stopped, the hair on the back of my neck standing and my scalp prickling. "They do, sir."

He came in sight, raising his arm and leaning his elbow against the living room entry. "Three thousand dollars," he said, then shook his head and grinned again. The glint in his eyes sharpened, and he reminded me of a laughing hyena ready to go in for the kill. "Three thousand dollars on a game you aren't going to play."

"Yes, sir. I'm playing for the Tigers now. You heard that, right?"

He furrowed his brow, and his voice lowered. "If you were a man, I'd beat you to a pulp—you hear?"

I nodded, thinking of how he'd talked about Preston. "I'd bet you would, sir, but I'm not. I'm just a kid. In fact . . . ," I said, "I still like playing with dolls, too."

His mouth snapped shut, and it looked like he would

explode. His neck flushed red, and he shook his head and walked away.

I turned toward the hall, and Preston stood there, staring at me. His expression was unreadable, just those big eyes studying my face. I realized he hadn't been there when I'd goaded Tom into betting more on the game. "Hey," I said.

He barely smiled, and it reminded me of Kermit the Frog. "Well, I suppose you're here."

I followed him to his room. He shut the door, then sprawled on the bed, staring at the ceiling. I stood, not knowing exactly what to do, then sat at the desk, swiveling the chair around. "You all right?"

"Yes."

"I mean, last night . . ."

He looked up, ignoring me as usual. "I'm assuming, based on the last hour of him yelling about it, that you talked Tom into betting three thousand dollars on the game you are not going to play."

I laughed, shaking my head. "I didn't talk him into anything. He talked himself into it just fine."

"Why?"

"Because he's a toad."

He scratched his head, then slowly patted down his hair. "You know what the difference is between being dumb and being stupid?"

I sat back in the chair, ready for another of his sermons. "Why can't you ever just answer a question? I asked you if you were okay. You could just answer the question. You know, like 'I'm fine' or 'I'm tired.' You know, like a normal person."

He went on. "Being stupid means you have the ability to understand why you're being stupid. Being dumb means you will never comprehend why you are dumb. Tom is dumb."

"He deserves what he gets, as far as I'm concerned."

He glanced at me. "If you saw a mentally challenged person pick up a loaded gun and fire it backwards, blowing his own face off, would you say he deserved it?"

"Oh, come on. I see what you're saying, but . . ."

Preston shrugged. "Tom wakes up every morning and shoots his face off and he doesn't even know it. And he's going to wake up every morning for the rest of his dumb life and do the same thing."

"He's mean."

Preston laughed. "Only if you take anything he says or does seriously."

"Will you answer my question now?"

"I already did."

I furrowed my brow.

"I'm not dumb, Brett."

"You could just have said you were all right. Pretty easy to do."

He sat up, sliding on the bed, his back propped up against the wall. "As far as last night, yes, I'm fine. And so are you. And as far as your friends making it clear to me that I am the official football team punching bag for the rest of the year, yes, I'm just fine with that, too."

"So you have a death wish."

"I didn't answer my phone when you called three times."

"Yeah, I noticed."

"I didn't want you to think I was avoiding you. I was just thinking."

"About what?"

"I was thinking it's a sign of paranoia to call somebody three times within three minutes."

"Are you answering another question?"

"No."

"I was worried is all." I shifted, swiveling the chair back and forth. "I just thought they might have gotten to you or something."

He shook his head. "They can't. You do remember I'm a superhero, right? I put an invisible shield of protection around myself this morning."

Of course I had no idea if he was being serious or not, but from the bit of sarcasm in his voice and the frog smile on his face, I guessed he was joking. I hoped he wasn't delusional. "Listen, this whole thing is a mess, Preston. I swear to God if they come after you, I'll get them."

"I'd rather have you take responsibility for making my cereal every morning. I hate pouring milk."

"I'm serious."

"So am I."

"Okay, whatever."

He slumped down, staring at the ceiling again. "How was your first day of school?"

"Fine. LC is pretty cool. You should think about transferring."

"I don't run from my problems."

My eyes bulged. "Hey, you were the one who put it in my head to transfer."

"You take everything so personally. But, then again, you're a very narcissistic person."

"What does that mean?"

"It means I'm buying you a dictionary. You didn't run from your problems—you solved them. I, on the other hand, have dealt with my kind of problems since the first day of kindergarten, and switching schools solves nothing." He smiled, putting his hands behind his head. "Fond memories, those. Dalton Richards was particularly good at pinning me down and farting in my face."

"You act like you were born to be picked on."

"I was."

"Don't be a victim."

He laughed. "Look who's talking."

I stood. "I gotta go. I'm going to try and talk to my dad."

He went back to staring at the ceiling. "See you later."

35

"If you really wanted to hurt me, you've done a good job." My dad sat on the back porch, watering the wilting potted plants from his chair.

I sat on the edge of the picnic table. "I wasn't trying to hurt you, Dad. I just want to play football."

He twisted the nozzle on the hose shut, letting it drop to the paving stones. "Coach Williams and I played through school together. We've been friends for over twenty-five years. He won't even return my calls."

I thought about what Preston said about the difference between being dumb and stupid. "What if I told you I was gay?"

He blinked, studied my face for a moment, then took a deep breath. "I, um, well, I guess I'd tell you I loved you. Can't say that I really agree with it, but . . ." He looked at me, his eyes questioning. "Is that what all of this is about?"

"Sort of. I'm not gay, Dad, but you'd accept me being gay more than you accept me playing for the Tigers. Or not playing at all."

"I just don't see what the issue was, Brett. I've done everything in my power to help you, and you rejected it all."

I realized then that no matter how much I tried to explain it, my dad, for all I loved him, got up every morning and shot himself in the face when it came to what he did for me. "What would Mom do if she were here?"

He sat back, staring over the backyard. We didn't talk much about her. After a moment, he said, "She'd tell me I was being too rough on you." He smiled, shaking his head. "She always said that I took things too far. That I got too involved in things. She was like the balance in my life. All the good things about her and all the bad things about me . . ." He went silent.

"You loved her, huh?"

He winced, leaning forward and putting his elbows on his knees. "She was the one for me." He took a deep pull from his beer, craning his neck up, then idly studied the bottle in his hands. "I've never even bothered looking for somebody else since she died."

"Is that why you drink yourself to sleep every night?"

The world stopped moving, the wind stopped blowing, the birds fell silent, and my dad wouldn't meet my eyes. "You think I—"

"I don't think you do—I know you do, Dad. And I know that every time you've hit me, you've been drunk. I also know that half the time you yell at me, you don't even remember it the next morning. You're a mean person, Dad.

You might wait until four o'clock every day to do it, but you're an alcoholic. You blew your knee out on the field. Then Mom died, and since then, there's been nothing to do but put every dream you ever had on my shoulders. And I'm sorry"—I shook my head as tears sprang to my eyes—"but you ruined football for me. You made me hate it. And I let you do it. And now you're pissed at me for trying to get it back."

He kept his head down, staring at his feet, his teeth clenched and his chin quivering.

I shook my head. "I'm sorry about your life, Dad, but I'm not paying for it anymore. I'm playing ball for me now. Not you. And if you can't at least accept that, I'd appreciate it if you'd stay out of it."

I sat there on the edge of the picnic table in silence, and he said nothing. Then his voice came, quiet, almost a whisper, throaty and thick with emotion. "Would you mind giving me some time? I'd appreciate that."

I nodded to his downturned head, then stood. "I love you."

He didn't reply.

36

I woke up to the sound of his voice through the walls. Bleary eyed, I glanced at my alarm clock. One-forty-five in the morning.

I sat up in bed and listened. It sounded like he was arguing with someone. I snagged a pair of shorts and put them on, then opened my door and looked down the hall. Dim light came from the living room, but his voice wasn't coming from there.

Tiptoeing down the hall, I listened as his voice, muffled gibberish, floated in from the kitchen. Then I realized he was out back and that his voice was coming through the open window. "I should have . . . ," he said, and then his voice trailed off.

I walked to the window, which looked out to the porch. There, in the darkness, my dad was on his hands and knees, head slung low, shoulders arched. He was talking to himself. At least a dozen empty beer bottles lay around him.

Chest heaving, sobbing, his words slurred. "I tried. I did. I can't do this alone, Kim. I can't. Please. Come back. Please. Why'd you leave? Please."

Over and over again he begged, rocking back and forth on his hands and knees, blindingly drunk, begging for my mother to come back. Blaming her for leaving. Cursing himself and God and his life.

I opened the back door, but he was oblivious to me. I knelt next to him and put my hand on his shoulder. He'd vomited, the stones covered in foodless beer and bile. "Dad, it's okay."

"She's gone and now he's gone, too. Everybody is gone," he mumbled.

I leaned down, looking at his face. Full of slobber and with drool hanging from his lips, his face wet with tears, he turned his head, seeing me for the first time. "Brett, it's time to get up. Practice starts soon. You can't be late, okay, buddy? Got to get up."

I'd never seen him this drunk. He had so much alcohol in him that reality didn't exist. Just whatever thoughts flitted through his saturated mind. I put my arm over his back, gripping under his arm and trying to get him upright. "Yeah, Dad. I'm ready, okay? Let's get you up now."

He resisted, shaking his head and trying to crawl away, but failing. When his hands hit the lawn, he lost whatever balance he had and thudded down, his cheek resting on the turf. He still mumbled, barely loud enough to hear, but I knew what he was saying.

I tried to get him up again, but he was deadweight. Barely conscious, arms down at his sides, half on the porch and half on the lawn, he was nothing more than an incredibly drunk and miserable beached whale. I knew I'd never get him in the house.

I went inside and came back armed with a blanket and a pillow. I lifted his head, put the pillow under his cheek, and spread the blanket over his passed-out body, then went back to bed thinking that my dad, for whatever he did, was a broken man, and it didn't have to do with a football.

37

Three days till the game with Shadle. Two more practices to prove my worth to the Tigers. After the morning practice, Coach Larson took me aside. "You fitting in well, Patterson?"

I took my helmet off. "You tell me, Coach."

"You're doing fine. You've got talent, but apparently it doesn't include math. Your grades transferred over as well as you."

I groaned, dreading the next few moments as much as I had with Coach Williams.

"Your new math teacher spoke to your old math teacher to find out more about what problems you were having, and she's getting a packet of extra credit ready for you. You get it all handed in by Friday before game time, you play."

I brightened. "Yessir. Will I start?"

"You focus on your grades, I'll focus on being the coach of this team. Got it?"

"Yessir."

He crossed his arms over his chest. "Your old teammates are hassling you."

"How'd you know?"

"I didn't know, but I know how the world works. How badly?"

"Nothing I can't handle, Coach. It's all good."

He clicked through his cheek. "You tell me if anything happens, and I'll get it straightened out with Coach Williams."

I said okay, but I definitely knew better than he did about Coach Williams. If anything, Coach Williams was giving them pointers on how to nail me to the wall.

After school, and after getting my math packet from Miss Boreline, who happened to be incredibly hot for a math teacher, I texted Preston, asking him if we could meet for tutoring. He texted back that he was going in for one of his counselor's counseling sessions, but that we could meet afterward.

I picked him up on the corner of Riverside and Division. He was talking to a homeless man who was holding a sign on the corner. It read "Why Lie? I Just Want a Beer."

After Preston hopped in, I pulled into traffic, and he immediately began his methodical ritual of cleaning my car. I turned down the radio. "That guy begging from you?"

He rolled a gum wrapper up and stuffed it in a Mountain Dew can. "No."

I glanced at him. " 'No.' Just 'No.' You don't know how to have a conversation, do you?"

He neatly folded up a Big Mac box. "What would you like to have a conversation about?"

I spoke slowly, like I was explaining something to a five-year-old. "Okay . . . You were talking to a bum. What were you talking about?"

"I asked him if he enjoyed being homeless."

"Yeah. I'm sure he loves it."

"He said he did. He referred to himself as a wanderer. He's been to every state. By the way, we can't go to my place today. After you left last week, Tom and Diane got in a huge fight. I heard him yelling about wanting to rip your face off and use it as toilet paper."

"Good to know I'm causing trouble in your family, too."

He shrugged. "I left after a while, but she kicked him out. He's supposed to be packing his stuff right now, and I don't feel like listening to his pity party."

I changed direction and headed toward my house, wholly uncomfortable with the thought of him seeing my room. I half expected him to have cleaned the entire thing by the time we were done with the math. "I didn't know he lived with you."

"He was in the process of slowly incorporating himself into living off my mom."

I drove, and we went on in silence, with Preston cleaning. He squished a napkin into the Mountain Dew can. "You know, if the superhero gig doesn't work out, you'd do great going to maid school."

"Do well, not good. And I don't think there is a maid school."

"You're my math tutor, not my English tutor."

"Seventy-three percent of all job applications have grammatical errors in them. Illiteracy is a major problem in America."

"I'll keep that in mind."

I pulled up in front of my house, my stomach squirming when I saw that my dad's car was in the driveway. I'd checked on him this morning before I left, and he was still breathing. I'd been doing that ever since the night he'd passed out, but otherwise I'd completely avoided him. I cleared my throat. "My dad isn't the coolest guy lately."

"What does that have to do with your grammar?"

"Nothing. It just might be sort of . . . Never mind. Come on."

Dad was nowhere to be found when we got inside, and I heaved a sigh of relief. "Well, here it is. My house," I said, ushering him as quickly as I could toward my bedroom. Once inside, I threw my pack on the bed. "I'll get some sodas for us. Be right back."

I almost ran to the kitchen and looked out the window, dreading to see my dad lying there, a beer-bloated corpse gathering flies. He wasn't, though, and I noticed that sometime in the last few days the porch had been completely cleaned. No bottles scattered about, the vomit hosed from the paving stones. I hurriedly grabbed two cans of Pepsi from the fridge and headed back to my room, seeing that Dad's office door was shut.

When I came back in, Preston was sitting at my desk, staring at nothing. I handed him a can. "Okay, my room, my rules. No cleaning."

He fidgeted, his eyes roaming over the ramshackle mess. "Okay."

I laughed. "I'll make you normal if it kills me."

"If normal is you, I'll kill myself instead."

I rummaged through my pack for the extra credit, found it, and tossed it to him. "Okay, chief, school me."

He caught it. "I have no Native American blood in—"

I cut him off. "Okay. Rule number one. We're in the normal zone. I know you're not an Indian, and I know you're not a chief. You don't have to take everything literally."

We were forty minutes into working when the knock came on my door. "Brett?"

I stood, walked over to the door, and opened it. The look on his face was different, but I couldn't tell why. "Hi."

"Can I come in?"

I hesitated, then opened the door wider. "Yeah."

He stepped in, looking at Preston. "Oh. I'm sorry. I didn't know you had anybody over. I just wanted to talk to you for a minute."

I swallowed, checking the clock on my nightstand. It was well into beer time. "No problem. This is Preston."

Dad nodded to him. He took a breath, then spoke. "Brett told me what happened with Lance Killinger and Tilly." He hesitated. "And that Coach Williams allowed it. It should have never happened, and I'm sorry."

Preston stared blankly at him, in typical form, then glanced at me. I could tell he was almost bursting to say something odd, but he didn't. "That's okay. It wasn't a big deal."

I knew then that for however blunt and literal Preston was, he was also polished at dealing with parents. My dad took another breath, uncomfortable, then went on. "I wanted to do this in private, but I learned some things today." He fished in his pocket and took out what looked like a poker chip, staring at it for a second. He handed it to me.

I looked at it, flipping it over. It had the number 24 etched into both sides. "What is it?" I asked.

He swallowed, his eyes flitting nervously from Preston to me. "It's a 24-hour Desire Chip. I went to my first Alcoholics Anonymous meeting this morning."

He could have shot me with a cannon and I wouldn't have been as blown away. I stared at the chip, then looked up to him. "Really?"

"Yes. I'm sorry, Brett." His eyes moistened just the slightest, and he looked away. "I'm an alcoholic. I've treated you poorly, and for all the wrong reasons. I love you," he finished, then looked to Preston. "It was nice meeting you. I'll order some pizza. It'll be on the counter." He walked out, closing the door behind him.

I stared at the chip in my hand, speechless. I'd learned two things in the last few weeks. The first was that my father was a broken and very lonely man. The second was that he wasn't dumb. He was a human being, not just a dad.

After a moment of stunning silence, Preston spoke. "I'm allergic to pepperoni."

38

Friday rolled around with two changes in my life. First off, my dad had thrown away the case and a half of beer in the garage refrigerator. We hadn't spoken about it since he'd told me he was going to AA, but things were different. He slept in his bed every night, instead of the recliner, and he was on edge. Nervous. Almost jumpy. He didn't talk a lot, but I could tell he was struggling. I cooked dinner both nights, we sat in the living room eating crappy food and watching TV, and I accepted the silence, knowing that his demons were considerably more demonic than mine. Not a single word was spoken about football, which I thanked God for.

Now that I was passing math, the only thing I had to worry about was not getting beaten to a pulp by half the Saxon team. And a small second thing.

The second thing was that Preston was cornered in the bathroom by Tilly and Killinger at lunch on Thursday.

They'd stripped him naked and stolen his clothes, leaving him shivering in a bathroom stall. Instead of cowering in there until he could be rescued, he'd blithely left the bathroom, walking down the halls naked among the laughter and shock of everybody until a teacher dragged him into a room.

I could've imagined Preston doing it, just like ignoring the eggs, but of course nothing was left to the imagination. They'd filmed it on their phones, and somebody uploaded it to the Internet. It went viral within hours, and Preston was instantly tagged "Nakedboy." I could have killed myself.

With the Shadle game in less than six hours, I should have been completely focused on football, but my head was full of one thing: Lance Killinger.

Twenty minutes before sixth period ended , I faked stomach cramps from a bad lunch and skipped out. I got my car and headed straight for the Hamilton parking lot, searching until I found Killinger's car, a tricked-out Honda Civic, lowered and with a spoiler big enough to fly a small plane. Typical Killinger.

Flashy, loud, and useless.

As I sat in my car waiting, I stared at the gaudy thing. No doubt his stereo system was worth more than my entire car, and I was tempted to grab the baseball bat from my trunk and go to work on it.

Fully into my fantasy of what a Louisville Slugger in my hands would make his car look like, I didn't notice him until he was almost to his car. I took my keys out of the ignition and opened the door.

He saw me, and for the slightest second, there was something on his face that I never figured I'd see. Fear. In an instant it disappeared, replaced with the contempt I was used to. He looked up, studying the sky, then wiped his forehead. "Hot today. Almost makes you want to"—he looked at me, then grinned—"strip down and go natural."

I stepped up to him. "It's gone too far. He doesn't have anything to do with this."

"Says you?"

"Yes."

He crossed his arms over his chest. "You can't do anything about it, Patterson."

I started toward him. I could end this, and I could end him. I would end him. His eyes widened for a second, and he jumped back, raising his hands and laughing. "Hold on, big boy, just hold on. Violence is never the way," he said, mocking me.

I knocked his hands away and grabbed him by his varsity jacket, slamming him against his car. My face was inches from his. Lance Killinger expected this. He expected me to lose my temper, and if I did, I'd lose a lot more, too, because he had power and he knew how to use it. He was untouchable because Coach Williams was the king of Hamilton High School, and the man would do anything or overlook anything in order to win games. Lance knew it, too. I stared at him, then let him go. He smiled, spreading his arms out, inviting me. "Come on, Patterson. What are you going to do? Hit me. Come on, pussy."

The difference between dumb and stupid. I nodded. "You know, Lance, I don't have to do anything. You're the one who has to figure out what to do."

He pointed at me. "You're the one, Patterson. You're dead. So is your little fag friend."

I smiled. "The only reason you're all butt-hurt is because you know."

He paused, staring at me. "Know what? I don't need to know anything other than you're mine."

I shrugged. "You know you're not as good as you say, Lance. You know that without me to catch for you, you're nothing but a second-string arm with a first-string mouth. And that hurts, doesn't it?"

The vein in his neck pulsed, and I could tell I'd hit my target. He worked his jaw muscles. "I can throw better—"

"No, Lance, you can't. That's why you're so pissed off at me. Because you know what you are. Deep down, you know. And the only thing you can do about it is to go after a fifteen-year-old dork because you're too chicken to come after me." I nodded, lowering my voice. "You're my bitch, Lance. You like that? Feel good?"

He jerked his jacket off, throwing it on the hood of the car. "Fine. You and me. Right now."

I smiled, looking around and gesturing. "Can't beat me on the field, so you want to try in a parking lot? You're sad, Lance."

He stood there, trembling he was so mad. "I can take you anywhere, anytime."

"Huh. Really?" I said, stuffing my hands in my pockets. "How about this, then. LC plays Hamilton next Friday. If we beat you, this ends. If you beat us, I'll meet you and Tilly anywhere you want."

Lance pursed his lips, thinking. Then he smiled. "Tilly and I are going to end you no matter what you do. No deal."

"Name your terms, then."

"If LC wins, it's over." He spat. "If we win, you quit football. Quit the Tigers."

"Preston is left alone either way, or no deal."

He laughed. "Deal. Get used to sitting at home, bitch. And by the way, it's only over after the game. Not until then. Watch yourself," he said, then put his jacket on, got in his car, and drove away.

As I watched him go, I exhaled, feeling like I'd held my breath for ten years. Lance Killinger was playing my game now. The only thing I had to do to win was stay one step ahead of him.

39

"Patterson! In my office!"

Lacing up my cleats, I hustled through the locker room. When I got to the office, Jordan Appleway and Dillon Yance, the starting wide receivers, were standing there. Jordan nodded when I walked in. Dillon shuffled his feet.

Coach Larson threw his pen on the desk. "I didn't say tomorrow, Patterson."

"Sorry, Coach," I said. Coach Larson was incredibly cool, but he expected you to do what he wanted before he even knew what he wanted you to do. I'd learned quickly enough that he expected two things at all times from his players: one hundred percent effort and psychic abilities.

He also didn't mince words. Sitting back in his chair, he nodded to me. "You'll be starting wide receiver with Appleway tonight. Right side."

I glanced at Dillon. He was a nice guy, and by the look on his face I could tell he was destroyed. "Thank you, Coach."

"You earned it. Keep earning it."

"Yessir," I said.

"You boys need an invitation to get out of my office?" he barked. "I've got to figure out how to get you knuckleheads to win this game."

I nodded, smiling.

Outside his office, Jordan slapped my shoulder. "Looks like you got it, babyface. Just try to keep up with me," he said, laughing.

I watched Dillon walk to his locker. "Yeah."

Jordan put fingers to lips and whistled. Everybody suiting up stopped what they were doing and looked at us. He raised his voice. "Y'all listen up! Looks like babyface learned how to play football since he got here. Boy is going to take his diapers off and be my wingman tonight, so be easy on him." He clapped me on the back again to the cheers of the team. He turned to me, jutting his chin at me and grinning. "So you think you're Stick, huh?"

"Some people think so."

He walked down the aisle, then turned, calling out, "Well, then I guess you are Stick."

We hit the field running, and I felt the electricity coursing through me again. The lights. The crowd. The announcer's voice blaring through the speakers. It felt like it'd been a whole season, not weeks, since I'd played. As I ran to our bench, I smiled, realizing that I *hadn't* played for over a season. Not the way I wanted to, anyway.

The only thing that had me on edge was my dad. Ever since I could remember, my dad had arrived early to every game, taking a spot four rows back at the fifty-yard line. I glanced up, hoping I wouldn't see him, but he was there. Yeah, things were better with him not drinking, but he still hadn't said a word to me about football.

The stadium was packed, and as we lined up for the most horrible rendition of the National Anthem I'd ever heard, Ben Lynch, standing next to me, bumped my arm. "Looks like you've got some fans."

I looked to where he was looking, and there, at the highest row of the stands on the Tigers' side, was the starting line of the Saxons, including Mike, Killinger, and Tilly, all wearing their jerseys. They also held poster boards.

Patterson = Traitor.
Stick doesn't stick.
Turncoat.
Quitter.
LC sucks.

I shook my head. Deal or no deal, Lance Killinger couldn't help himself. But the main thing I cared about was that they lay off Preston. The other thing was that Mike, my best friend for years, was one of them standing up there holding a sign.

After the anthem and the coin toss, Coach Larson called me over. He put his hands on my shoulder pads, staring at me through my face mask. He nodded to the stands. To the Saxons. "I don't care why you left, Brett, because it doesn't matter. The right here and the right now matter. Focus on the field. The game."

The shadow lifted, and the electricity came back. I was playing for all the right reasons, and Coach knew it.

We lost the toss, and as we were about to take the field, Jordan jogged up to me, slapping my helmet. "You a Tiger?"

"You bet."

He smiled through his face mask. "We got you, buddy."

Shadle was playing zone, not man on man, which was my strong suit because I could confuse them, and I was excited. I'd watched tapes of the cornerbacks and safeties and I knew their weaknesses. Give me the ball and I could take them. I knew I could, and between Jordan and me, I knew without a doubt we were the strongest team in the league. Adrenaline flowed through me like quicksilver.

We took the field, and the stadium quieted as we huddled for the first play. Fans chomped down on hot dogs, drank their sodas, and watched. The cheerleaders finished their cheer, and Ben should have called out the play in the huddle. He didn't. His sardonic smile and easy drawl came like a greased pig out of a chute. "Looks like some people don't know whose house they're in." Then he called out the play. He went on, looking me in the eye and talking to the guys. "We got some schooling to do. Let's do it." Then he broke huddle.

Nobody went to position. Every Tiger on the field lined up, facing the stands. Then they raised their right arms, pointing to the top row, to my old teammates. Silence reigned in the stadium. Soon, every Tiger on the sidelines had turned to face them, pointing. Three thousand faces in the stadium stared at the Saxons.

Slowly, a voice at a time, the crowd started booing. In

another ten seconds, you couldn't hear yourself talk over the noise.

My old teammates tried to slink down the aisles and disappear, but I saw a group of over twenty guys from LC meet them halfway up. Security swarmed. I laughed. Ben slapped me on the back, yelling over the crowd, "Let's play some ball, Stick."

I found out soon enough what Coach Larson was all about. Shadle had me pinned to the ground from the start. They'd based their whole defense on Coach Larson using me to whip their asses. I was double-teamed every play, but I'd studied them. I knew them. I knew their play.

Coach Larson completely ignored me.

By the second half, I'd only held the ball twice, each time a diversion to put Shadle back on to me. Jordan was having a stellar game, and Coach Larson played a running game against a team that had planned a passing game. Their zone defense was left with basically chasing me around the field while Jordan and the running backs were raising hell on them.

I couldn't even bear to look up in the stands at my dad.

I'd gone through hell to be here. I'd made the right choices, worked my ass off, proved myself . . . and Coach wasn't using me.

Back on the field before third quarter, I stepped up to him. "Coach?"

He turned to me, saying nothing, waiting.

"Did I do something wrong? I mean, I thought I showed you what I can do. I earned it, but you're not using me."

His jaw snapped shut, and his eyes glinted. "You look like a wide receiver to me, Patterson."

I blinked. "Yessir."

He worked his jaw muscles. "So, you're not the coach of this team, then?"

"Nosir. I'm sorry, I just . . ."

He pointed. "Then get your ass on that bench. You're out until I say you're in. You got that?"

I hadn't been benched before. Ever. "Yessir."

He furrowed his brow. "I said now. Get out of my face."

I sat on the bench, my helmet planted between my feet on the turf, for the entire third quarter, watching Dillon struggle through the plays. I could almost feel my dad's eyes burning holes through me. I'd screwed up. I'd failed, and I was a fool. I had nearly every state record under my belt, and . . . nothing. I sat and watched the game, and my father's judgment ripped through me like wildfire.

We were down three by the fourth quarter. Jordan and Ben ignored me, but their eyes didn't. Every time they came off the field, they looked at me. I couldn't tell what they were thinking, but there was a question in both of their expressions.

Just before the fourth started, Coach walked up to me, jabbing a finger in my face. "Tell me what football is to you, Patterson."

"It's about doing what you love, sir."

He shook his head, narrowing his eyes. "If life was that easy, I'd own an island in the South Pacific and sit drinking girly drinks with umbrellas in them. I also wouldn't have to deal with a bunch of snot-nosed idiots like yourself every damn day. It's about being a part of something that's bigger than you, and loving being a part of something that's bigger than you. It's not about a game, Patterson, it's about life."

I nodded. "Yessir."

"This team does not exist for you, and as long as you don't see it that way, you'll sit on my bench. You got that?"

My stomach shrank. "Yes, Coach."

He leaned down, bringing his face to mine. "I don't give a single damn about what one person does on this field. I give a damn that when my players leave this school, they know what being a part of something is. Are you ready to play some football, Patterson?"

"Yessir."

"Are you ready to be a part of this team?"

"Yessir."

He grinned, nodding. "Then I'll coach this team and you'll play for it. Get off that bench and do your job."

I did. And the ball never touched my hands. I couldn't figure it out. Ben called run play after run play, handing the ball off every time as we ground our way down the field. Shadle had turned their full attention to the run game, and I was all but being ignored.

Still down by three with seconds left on the clock. We'd come up short, with the ball at the forty-yard line. As we huddled, Ben smiled. "Stick, you ready to do something besides run in circles?"

I nodded.

"Quick Ace 38."

I blinked.

He went on. "They'll be expecting the ball going long to Jordan. We got one shot at this."

As we lined up, I took a breath. Ben looked up and down the line, then called the snap. Jordan and I were off the line like lightning, heading downfield as Shadle ran a blitz toward Ben. With Jordan streaking down the sideline and staying wide, I stopped ten yards out, spinning on a dime. The cornerback on me didn't see it coming, and I was completely open. Just as Ben was swallowed by green and yellow uniforms, he threw the ball.

I caught it, feeling the leather slap my hands, and I ran. I ran like I'd never run in my life, sweeping past the cornerback, feeling the adrenaline pump through me. Everything slowed down, just like it always did when I had the ball. I had no conscious thought, just clear shapes on the field. Patterns. Avenues to run, shapes to avoid.

And I ran. The defensive backs turned from the end zone, zeroing in on me as I headed toward them. Jordan sprinted toward me as I spun around a defender, feeling his hands slip from me, trying to rip the ball from my arms.

With ten yards to go, I saw it coming. Saw the goal line, saw the defensive back running to intercept me. There was no way I could avoid him, and I readied myself for one hell of a hit, hoping I could smash through him and into the end zone.

Just as the guy dove toward me, Jordan, steps behind, launched himself, diving toward us and nailing the guy full on at the shoulders. I heard the crunch, almost felt it I was so close, and heard air leave lungs.

Then I was in.

We won.

40

"Coach Larson, right?"

My dad was on the sidelines now, having come down from the stands. He held his hand out to Coach, and I was having a nervous breakdown. This is where he'd light into the coach, ripping him up one side and down the other for benching his son. Coach Larson shook his hand. "Yes."

My dad nodded. "I'm Brett's father, Stuart."

Coach nodded. "Nice to meet you, Mr. Patterson."

I looked around nervously, seeing too many people still milling around after the game. I tried to make eye contact with my dad, but he was focused on Coach. There would be a scene. I held my breath as my dad spoke. "Fantastic game. I haven't seen that in years."

I was stunned. What? Fantastic? How?

Coach smiled. "Thank you, Mr. Patterson."

Dad laughed, shaking his head. "They had no idea what to

do. That's some old-school tactics. Team play. Not star play. You used Brett perfectly."

Coach laughed. "Probably won't work again, but I saw the opportunity and took it. Brett is a talented player."

He nodded, glancing at me. "He is. He's a good boy."

Coach adjusted his baseball cap. "I'm going to tell you, Mr. Patterson, that what those boys from Hamilton did tonight is unacceptable. I'll be lodging a formal complaint with the league for conduct unbecoming off the field."

Without hesitation, my dad replied, "Brett is strong. He'll be fine." They shook hands again, and my dad faced me. "Good game, son. I'll see you at home."

Then he was gone, winding his way through the crowd and leaving me wide-eyed and wondering what had just happened.

41

I closed the door behind me. My dad wasn't in his usual spot after a game, which was always in front of the TV with a beer in his hand, watching the tape. Clatter came from the kitchen. I walked in, and he stood at the counter next to the sink, getting plates down. He turned. "Hey, son."

He'd stopped for Chinese takeout, which was also unheard of because it was expensive and didn't fit my diet.

"Hi."

Opening the fridge, he took out a gallon of milk. "You hungry?"

I smiled. "Starving."

He put out two glasses. "Well, set the plates and we'll dig in."

I did so as he placed the white boxes on the kitchen table. I couldn't remember the last time we'd eaten at the table. We sat and dished out egg foo yung, almond chicken, rice, and whatever that slimy vegetable dish was that I loved so much.

Things were still weird, and we ate for a minute or so in silence. He finally spoke. "Funny how there's a bit more money around when somebody isn't spending it on beer."

I looked at him for a second, then laughed, swallowing a huge chunk of chicken. "Yeah."

He ate, then cleared his throat. "That was a nice run, Brett. I'm proud of you."

It was so natural for me to expect, and wait, for him to cut to the chase. Next would come what I should have done. What I'd screwed up. What I should work on. Why I had been benched. "Thanks."

Taking a drink of his milk, he wiped his mouth. "You know, I was thinking that maybe we could do something tomorrow."

I looked up at him. Just the two of us, sitting alone and eating, was weird. He was weird. I wondered if he was trying a new tactic with his same old game. I couldn't get it into my head that things might be changing. "Oh yeah?"

"Yeah, I saw this preview for a movie. Something about a cop that saves the world from some alien attack?"

"Yeah. *Armageddon Is Now.* It looks pretty good."

He took a bite. "Well, maybe we could go."

The last time we'd done anything on a Saturday afternoon that didn't have to do with football or me paying the price for what I'd done wrong the night before was when I was in diapers. In fact, I couldn't remember ever going to the movies with him. He hated them. "Really?"

"Yeah. It looks good. You in?"

I smiled. "Yeah. That sounds great."

"Good. Then it's a date."

I stared at him as he got up, clearing his plate. "Hey, Dad?"

"Yeah?"

"I don't get it."

He stopped, looking at me. "Get what?"

"Was Coach Larson punishing me for something? Was it some sort of test?"

He turned, leaning against the counter and looking at me. "I think that's something you should take up with him. What I do know is that I'd like to go see a movie with you tomorrow. Maybe we'll grab a burger afterward, huh?"

I sat, frowning into my plate. My dad's body was the one invaded by aliens. "Yeah, sure."

Just then the doorbell rang. Dad put his plate in the sink. "I'll get it. Finish up," he said, walking out. I heard him open the door, and I heard a familiar voice.

"Hello, Stuart. We need to talk."

It was Coach Williams.

I listened to my dad. "About what, Don?"

Coach's voice was insistent and authoritative, as usual. I figured the guy was born with a coach's whistle stuck up his butt. "About Brett."

I heard my dad let Coach in, and they sat. "Brett? Can you come in here, please?" my dad called.

I picked up my plate, setting it on the counter and walking to the living room. Coach Williams gave me an unblinking stare. "Hello, Brett. I was hoping to have a private conversation with your father," he said, completely ignoring what my dad had just said.

I stood there, not knowing what to do.

My dad cut in. "Have a seat, son."

I did, sitting in one of the recliners. Coach Williams worked his jaw muscles, staring at me for a moment, his blond crew cut glistening with gel. "Okay, then. I'm here to talk about this nonsense with the team. With the Tigers. We've got to straighten things out, Stuart."

"We need to figure things out, Don? What exactly do we need to figure out?"

Coach Williams blinked, then leaned forward, putting his elbows on his knees and clasping his hands together. "Listen, Stuart, whatever Coach Larson did to sway Brett over to the Tigers is against league rules. There could be big trouble for them. They'd have to forfeit the game Brett played in tonight, which would take them out of contention for the playoffs. That's why I waited to talk to you until now. And with Brett back at Hamilton, I could take them all the way to state again. That's all I'm saying, and I think you know my thinking. This whole thing was a big misunderstanding, and if Brett comes back, I'm sure we could work everything out."

Silence, with my dad studying his face. Then he spoke. "We've known each other for almost twenty-five years, Don."

He smiled. "Yes, we have. Good years, too."

"Did you watch Brett and his friend get assaulted by Killinger and Tilly?"

Coach shook his head. "Come on, Stuart, you know boys will be boys. Tensions were high. They need to get things out of their systems."

"So, Brett should lie and say he was recruited by Larson, get them canned for the year. We should ignore two of your football players committing assault on my son, along with seriously hurting a skinny freshman. And we could win state. Is that what you're saying, Don?"

Coach shook his head again. "No, no, no. It wouldn't be that way. You're not understanding. Brett wouldn't need to—"

My dad interrupted, looking at me. "Brett, I'm very sorry. You were right, and I should have seen this. I should have listened to you." His eyes went to Coach Williams. "Don, I do understand. You're welcome to leave my home."

Coach Williams stared, in shock. "Stuart, come on. I'm not saying that Brett—"

Dad stood. "Get out of my home. Now."

Coach Williams stood, anger flushing his face. "You were always the weak one, Stuart. Always. And now you're throwing your own son's life down the drain. He'll end up being just another loser."

I'd never seen my dad so intense. He stepped up to Coach, eye to eye, then suddenly grabbed the front of his shirt with both fists. His voice was low, dripping with venom. "You don't say that about my boy. You *understand* what I'm saying? Because if you don't, I'll show you." Then he released him, shoving him back.

Coach raised his hands. "Whoa, Stuart, calm down. Come on, there's no need for this."

My dad nodded. "No, there's not. You heard what I said. Get out before I throw you out."

Dad and I stood looking as Coach shut the door. I couldn't

believe what I'd just seen. After a moment, my dad nodded to himself, some thought agreed upon in his head. He looked at me, then smiled. "He was always an asshole. Let's see what's on the tube, huh?"

I grinned. "Yeah. Let's."

42

Saturday morning, I got on my computer with dread after several people had texted me about Preston being Nakedboy. Clicking on the YouTube icon, I dragged up the video. Several copies had been made, but there was a new one, which was definitely higher quality. Almost professionally done. Somebody had put some time into it, because they'd made almost like a music video of Nakedboy walking down the halls, complete with what they called the Naked Dance. Over two million hits.

At the end of the video, I cringed. They were offering Nakedboy T-shirts for sale. For $9.99, you could be wearing a shirt emblazoned with a full-color picture of Preston walking naked down the hall. His genitals were blurred, but his face and his pale, scrawny body were plain as day. Above the picture, "NAKEDBOY!" was printed across the chest of the shirt. Below was "Do the Naked Dance!"

I grabbed my keys and rushed into the living room. My dad was sitting at the kitchen table reading the paper. I called to him, "I've got to go, Dad. Something came up. Can we catch the movie later?"

"You all right?"

"Yeah. Just something. I'll let you know, okay?"

"You got it. Just give me a buzz."

I opened the door. "Bye."

In my car, I hit the steering wheel. I'd hoped beyond hope that the interest in Preston would fade. Most things like that did. But if anything, it was bigger. Viral. I could kill Lance Killinger.

At the entry to Preston's apartment, I buzzed the intercom. "Yes?"

"Mrs. Underwood? It's Brett. Is Preston there?"

"Come on up. I'll tell him you're here."

As the elevator opened, I did a double take. Jordan Appleway stood there. I furrowed my brow. "You know Preston?"

He cocked an eye at me. "Who?"

"Preston Underwood. He goes to Hamilton."

"The kid upstairs? Yeah, we've met a couple of times. Seems nice enough. You know him?"

"Yeah. He's one of my friends. You live here?"

He laughed. "You don't think a black kid can have money, Stick?"

"No. No. You just surprised me is all. I thought for a second you were here visiting Preston."

He slapped my shoulder, laughing. "Joke, buddy. I use the black thing all the time. Hey, take it easy." He walked to the doors, turning. "We'll see you later, babyface."

Mrs. Underwood answered the door. "Hello, Brett. How are you?"

I wanted to blurt out that I felt like killing myself because I'd managed to ruin her son's life, but I didn't want to be overdramatic. "I'm fine. Thanks."

"Preston is in his room," she said, walking into the kitchen and leaving me.

I walked down the hall to Preston's door. I knocked.

"Enter," came the droll reply.

I rolled my eyes, opening the door. He was lying on his bed, staring at the ceiling. He held a tennis ball in one hand, squeezing it. I shut the door, playing it cool. "Hey. What's up?"

"The sky. Elevators. Flagpoles. An estimated three hundred billion stars in our galaxy."

I walked across the room and slumped down in his computer chair. "You know Jordan Appleway?"

"No."

"He lives in this building. Plays wide receiver on the Tigers with me."

"Oh, him. Yeah. I know him."

I looked out the window, across the city. "I am so not right with this."

"With me knowing your teammate?" he said, then tossed the ball up, trying to catch it above him. It came down, bouncing off his hand and hitting him in the face. He picked it up again.

"No. The video. Haven't you seen? There's like four versions now. The worst has over two million hits."

"I know."

Exasperated, I shook my head. "Well, there's got to be something we can do. Get them banned. Something. You're smart. We could hack it or something."

"Why?" he said, trying to throw the ball up again. This time it hit him in the eye.

"*Why?* They're selling shirts now, that's why! And you know that by Monday people at school will be wearing them."

"I know."

"And that doesn't bug you? You're not going to be able to go outside for months without people laughing at you. If ever. Jesus, it might go national, if it hasn't already."

"Have you always been concerned about what other people think? Maybe you should see my counselor."

"I'd like to find out who made it. I'd kill them."

He turned his head, looking at me. "Why are you so upset about this?"

"Why? First of all, because it's wrong. Second, it's just a bit humiliating for you, wouldn't you agree?"

He threw the ball up again. It hit him in the shoulder. "I've never been ashamed of my nakedness," he said, then sat up. His hair was sticking out at all angles. He stood and walked over next to me. Touching the mouse to his computer, the screen flashed, coming alive. Then he walked back to his bed, lying back down again.

I glanced at the screen, ready to lay into him for not being pissed off about the whole thing, like any normal person should. Then I stopped, studying the screen. It was some sort of statement from Holyoake Industries, based in Los Angeles, California. "What's this?"

"Order tracking."

I looked closer: 44,366 orders for item number 324565. "You own a business?"

"No. I contracted the shirts out to Holyoake."

I frowned, looking at the screen again. "Shirts? Wha—" I blinked. "No way."

"Yeah way. My out-of-pocket expense for each one is $4.17. I'm making a profit of $5.82 for every order. And 44,366 times $5.82 equals $258,210.12. That's how much money I've made in two days. Of course, that doesn't take into consideration taxes, licenses, copyrights, and—"

I cut in. "YOU'RE selling the Nakedboy shirts?"

He looked at me like I was an idiot, which apparently I was. "Of course. When I saw how poor the quality was on the first video, and how popular it was, I made the new one. Pretty good, huh? I think I did a good job with the music and stuff. I even made up the dance. People like stupid dances like that."

I was speechless. He'd just made over two hundred and fifty grand on the backs of his victimizers, and God knew how much more he'd make over the next few weeks until it died down. I stared at him as he threw the tennis ball up and it bounced off his forehead. Brilliant. He was brilliant. But he couldn't catch a ball for the life of him.

It took a moment for it all to sink in, but when it did, I sat back and laughed. And I kept laughing. I couldn't stop, and the best irony was that Lance Killinger, who wanted nothing more than to hurt him, had just made Preston Underwood the wealthiest fifteen-year-old kid I'd ever known.

I realized Preston was staring at me. "What?" I asked.

"Why are you laughing?"

I slapped my leg. "Dude, you are so out there, such a freak. But you know what? You're awesome. You're the most awesome human being I've ever known. I can't believe you."

"I am pretty cool."

"Does your mom know?"

He nodded. "She had to sign off on some issues since I'm a minor, and she lent me the start-up cost. Things have gone pretty smoothly, though, especially when taking into consideration that I needed to find a manufacturer that could almost immediately begin printing and distributing them."

"Wow. You're rich. You know that, right?"

"I suppose so. My calculations, based on the number of hits versus the percentage of orders, should top out at around four hundred thousand dollars or so before it fades. It's hard to gauge how long consumer interest will last until they latch onto another useless thing to spend money on. There are orders from all over the world, though."

I scratched my head, still trying to take it all in. "Hey, you want to go to a movie today? My dad and I are going."

"I take it he is still not being drunk?"

"Dry as a bone," I said, relating the story about the game, and about Coach Williams coming over.

He listened, then got up. "That's cool, Brett. I saw the game."

I narrowed my eyes. "How? It wasn't on television this week."

"Well, they have these things called buses. You get on one, drop money into a machine, and a man or woman driving the bus will take you to your destination."

"You actually came to the game?" I said, surprised that he'd watch something he hated.

"No. I just thought I'd tell you I did for no reason."

"Okay, fine, sorry. But why did you go?"

He shrugged. "I'm sort of new at having friends, but I thought they supported each other's interests."

I studied his face, and of course couldn't read anything into it. For all I knew he was joking, but he sounded dead serious in his weird dead-serious way. "Thanks."

"You're welcome. And yes, I'll go to the movie with you guys. I'm sure it will be mundane and have little or no plot value, but I've decided to assimilate myself into mainstream culture more often. And I like popcorn."

43

Yes, I'm a stalker. I couldn't help myself. I sat in my car, parked way back in the corner of the dark lot, waiting. We'd had a great time at the movies the day before, and of course Preston had been bluntly honest about it not having any value other than spending two hours watching unrealistic special effects and incredibly poorly written dialogue that complemented a plot that a third grader could have come up with. My dad agreed wholeheartedly, and they'd laughed about it.

I thought it was an awesome flick.

The one thing predictable about Preston was that there had to be an order to everything he did. A pattern. He was too obsessive-compulsive to not have everything in his life under control, and that's why I was waiting for him.

He counted under his breath when he climbed stairs. He knew exactly how many stairs there were from the first to the second floor of the school. Everything he owned was alphabetized, from the sodas in his mini-fridge to the color of the shirts in his closet, starting with B for blue. He told me that for the most efficient tooth brushing, thirty-two strokes covered it nicely and reduced the buildup of plaque by fifteen percent in most cases. He left his condo every weekday at exactly 6:47 a.m.

So I sat. And I knew I'd see him. Midnight came and went. At 1:15, I smiled, watching as a shadowy figure left the entry to his building. The avenging Nakedboy was on the prowl tonight, and I was going to follow him.

As I hopped out of my car and started trailing him, I wondered why I was doing what I was doing. He was a friend, yeah, but it was more than that. Something about the kid made me want to watch out for him. Almost like a little brother—which he would reject if I ever said it to him. I was learning that Preston, for all outward appearances, could take care of himself better than most people I knew. Including myself.

But I still wondered.

Preston walked northwest, away from the downtown area and toward the river. Just before an old railroad bridge, he left the street and made his way across a vacant field, coming up behind a row of low-roofed buildings. At one end was a parking lot with three or four cars in it, and he stopped in the shadows at the edge. The end building looked like a small bar or club, but I couldn't see the sign because of the angle. Just neon splashing the night.

I watched as Preston took his pants and hoodie off, revealing his superhero costume underneath. Then he crouched beside a bush.

I stepped to a tree, trying to blend in as I watched. Either Preston chose random parking lots to watch, which wouldn't surprise me, or he was waiting for something. Or someone.

At two o'clock, good old Tom came walking around the corner of the building, keys jangling in his hand as he staggered to the lot. I groaned. Why would Preston be waiting for him? His mom had dumped him, and as far as I knew, that was that. He was out.

Tom reached his car, which was no more than ten feet from Preston. As the fat lawyer punched the key fob and went to open the door, Preston leaped up and ran toward him awkwardly, his cape flying behind him. Tom heard him just at the last moment, and he turned, giving a startled yelp when he saw the incredibly unintimidating skinny superhero charging at him. Just as Tom raised his hands, Preston's arm jabbed toward Tom's face. I saw a blue spark come from Preston's hand.

In the next second, Tom was flat as a board on the ground, groaning. Without hesitation, Preston knelt down and fastened a pair of handcuffs around his wrists. Then he sat him up against the side of his car, rifling through his pockets and taking the man's phone from him.

Creeping closer, I got to within a few feet of them. Tom was still groaning, his feet splayed in front of him, his wrists shackled and sitting in his lap.

Preston spoke. "I saw the marks. Confronted her. She told me."

Tom blinked, furrowing his brow at the voice, peering at the mask-covered face. "Preston?" he said groggily.

Preston crouched down in front of the man. "You hit her."

This wasn't payback for Tom being a jerk—this was real payback.

Tom struggled with the handcuffs. "You let me go right now, you little fucking weirdo. I swear to God . . ."

Preston flicked the Taser against his face once more, and Tom tightened, spasming uncontrollably for a few seconds, gasping and blubbering. Preston went on. "You hit my mother."

Tom was breathing heavily, his sweaty jowls shining in the dim. "Okay, okay. I'm sorry. What do you want? Money? I'll give you money. Whatever. Just let me go."

"It doesn't work like that, Tom. Let me explain," Preston said, then placed the Taser directly on Tom's forehead. "I want you to put yourself in jail, Tom."

"What? Your mother didn't press charges. She won't. It's done, and I'm gone."

Preston shook his head. "In the state of Washington, the victim doesn't need to press charges if the police determine a domestic act of violence has been committed." He took Tom's phone, sliding it open and pressing an icon. Light splashed across Tom's face. "Tom, you know the right thing to do, and you might be able to be a somewhat less than disgusting human being if you do it. I'll help you. You should confess to hitting my mother. Please be specific with time, date, names, and location. I'll record it on your phone."

Tom struggled against the handcuffs. "You can't be serious. I'm an attorney, for God's sake."

Preston nodded, his cape shifting in the breeze. "Then you know I'm correct about the law."

Tom shook his head, looking at Preston's costume. "I'm

not confessing to anything. I'll have you jailed for kidnapping and assault, you freak. Release me now."

Preston lowered the Taser and took something from one of the slots on his utility belt. "My mom isn't very good at math, Tom. You know that. What you didn't know is that I handle all of her finances because I'm one of those smart people you think you're smarter than." He held up the items in his hand. "These three checks that you forged her signature on would result in much more serious charges than misdemeanor domestic violence. They equal over a thousand dollars, which I think is a felony. But I'm not an attorney. Perhaps you can give me some legal advice. Is it a felony, Tom?"

Tom sighed, then leaned his head back against the side of the car, staring up at the night. I realized I was watching a master at work.

Tom blustered, "Okay. Fine. I'll do it, but I'll watch you tear those checks up after I do."

Preston held the phone up. "Okay. Start. Make sure you use your lawyer lingo. We need it official-sounding."

Tom groaned, then began, "I, Tom Clarkston, committed an act of domestic violence . . ."

A few minutes later, after the recording was finished and the checks had been destroyed, Preston unlocked Tom's hands and held the Taser up. "You did the right thing, Tom."

Tom sneered, rubbing his wrists. "Give me my phone."

Preston shook his superhero head. "I'll be taking it to the police station and showing them the video. I'm sure they'll be asking you to come down and pick it up after I show it to them."

Tom clenched his teeth. "You're nothing but a—"

Preston cut him off. "Yes, I am, Tom. I'm nothing but a freaky little weirdo. But I'm also better than you, and I'm smarter than you will ever be. You shouldn't have hit my mother."

As I followed Preston back to his place, he suddenly turned around. "And you say I'm odd. Do you follow other people around, or just me?"

I rolled my eyes. "I was going to . . . ," I began, but stopped. "That was amazing, Preston."

He shrugged. He'd put his pants and hoodie back on, and his stance was typical Preston. "Unfortunate, but necessary."

"Are you really going to show them the video?"

"Of course. And I know they'll visit my mom, too. She might not have called the police on him, but she values authority too much. She'll tell the truth if they ask her."

We walked along.

As we neared his place, he said, "Lance Killinger came to my apartment this afternoon."

I looked at him. "He knows where you live?"

"I don't have a batcave, Brett. We're listed in the directory."

"What did he do?"

"He told me about your stupid deal. And that he has to leave me alone for it to work."

"Yeah. That's right."

He stopped, facing me. "Do you know what you're doing?"

"I hope so."

"He's coming after you. They are."

"Yeah. I can handle it."

He shook his head. "They're not just going to beat you up, Brett. They're going to hurt you badly enough that you can't play. So they win."

"I know," I said, and we walked.

We reached the parking lot a few minutes later. Preston hitched his pack up higher. "If you want to follow me around some more, be here at nine-thirty tomorrow night."

"Sure. Why, though?"

He smiled. "I'm not as lonely as you think. See ya."

I woke up Monday morning with five days on my mind. Five days until we played Hamilton. Five days of watching my back. I didn't know when it would come, or how many there would be, but I knew Killinger would get me when I least expected it.

I'd had dreams of broken fingers. A dislocated shoulder. Of being stomped and beaten. Preston was right. This wasn't a vendetta, it was Lance Killinger wheeling toward a goal, and I was in the way. I also saw Mike's face leering down at me, replaced with his fist screaming toward me. But there was only one thing to do. I couldn't hide. I wouldn't hide. I'd do what I set out to do. I just needed to be smarter than him.

Getting up from my bed, I walked to my dresser, picking up the business card. I stared at it, remembering that day in our living room. The day that exploded everything in my life. I dialed the number.

"Silvia," the sleepy voice answered.

"Mr. Silvia, this is Brett Patterson. I'm sorry to call so early. We met a while ago—in Spokane. I played for the Hamilton Saxons, and you came up for a game."

His voice brightened. "Yes, Brett. How are you?"

"Well, I'm actually great. I'm playing," I said, and I explained in soft terms what had happened. We spoke for a few more minutes, and after I hung up, I walked to the kitchen, where my dad was reading the paper.

He looked up. "Hey, son. You were out late last night."

I swallowed. Busted. Years of him passed out by nine had given me freedom in the past, not that I'd done anything more than go to the store to sneak an ice cream or soda, and I still wasn't used to him being sober and aware. "Yeah, I met up with Preston."

He eyed me. "I suppose you're old enough to take care of yourself, but I'd appreciate a heads-up when you're going to be out that late. Everything okay?"

I sat down, surprised once again. It was like he was a completely different person. "Not really. Can I tell you something?"

He set the paper down.

I looked at the surface of the Formica table, hoping I'd find some sort of symbolic answer in the speckles. "Preston dresses up like a superhero and goes out at night, stopping crime. He gets the crap kicked out of him," I said, explaining the black eye, the bruises, and what had happened at the convenience store.

When I finished, my dad studied my face, most likely waiting for the punch line. When it didn't come, he bit his cheek, thinking. "I suppose it's a bit odd."

I shook my head. "No, actually, it makes sense," I said, explaining about Preston's father being murdered in front of him and how he felt guilty about it.

Dad took a sip of coffee and tapped his finger on the table. "Your mother was on bed rest for the entire time of her pregnancy—I think I've told you that before," he said, his voice getting thick. He looked at me for a moment, then went on. "She was going crazy, you know? All day, every day, in bed for months. I tried to make her happy, but she was miserable. I couldn't imagine it, but she held up pretty well. Then, two months before her due date, she'd had enough. She begged me to take her out. Just one night. Just a couple of hours, you know? So I did. She picked a movie, and I took her." He continued looking out the window. "*Love, Forever*," he said, nodding to himself. "It had come out just the day before, so I walked her to the car and drove her downtown. She loved it. She laughed and she cried, and I hated every minute of it because it was a horrible movie, but even more so because I was so worried about her." He stopped, and I saw tears gather in his eyes. "After the movie, we came home, and an hour later she had her first contraction. Four hours after that, I saw you being born. So tiny. Helpless. You were so premature the doctors said you might not live. . . ."

I swallowed. "Dad, you don't have to do this. It's okay."

He cleared his throat. "As they rushed you to the intensive care unit, your mom never took her eyes from me. She was so scared, Brett. Bleeding so badly. The doctors and nurses worked hard, but she knew. She knew our time was over, and she just looked at me as I held her hand. She never

202

said a word, and she didn't have to. Then she was gone. Just like that. Gone." He stopped, and a tear ran down his cheek. He looked at the table. "I killed her, Brett. If I'd kept her home, she'd be here right now. She'd know you."

Tears streamed down my face, and I bit my lip. My dad didn't cry. I'd never seen him shed a tear over anything. "You didn't. It just happened."

He wiped his tears away and looked at me. "I went to see that movie every day until it left the theaters, Brett. I saw it thirty-six times. I saw it to remind me of her, and how wonderful she was, and to punish myself. And when I hated myself enough over it, I started drinking to forget it." He said, and his face hardened. "Your friend will always feel that guilt, Brett. Nobody will ever take it away. But if it gets ahold of him, it'll ruin his life, just like I ruined mine. If there's anything you can do to help him, do it."

45

I met Preston at nine-thirty, wondering what he had in store for the night. He had his backpack, and I fell in line with him as he walked. "So, I never really asked. What do you call yourself?"

"Homo sapiens."

"No. Like, your name."

"Preston."

"No, like, your superhero name. Captain Weirdo or something."

"I thought about Commander General Death Seeker of the Knights of the Shining Galaxies, but it was too long to stencil on my chest, and most people wouldn't remember it."

I rolled my eyes. "Are you ever not the most difficult person in the world to talk to?"

"When are you ever not a tool? Do I have a name? Do

I need a name to do this? Do you have a football name?" There was an awkward silence for a moment, and then he went on. "Okay, so you have a football name, but personally I think it's a stupid concept."

I kicked a rock and watched it skip away in the darkness. I had no idea where we were going. "So just Preston, then?"

"You think this is stupid."

"Yeah, I do, but not because it's weird. It's stupid because it'll get you killed."

"The police came to the apartment today and got a statement from my mom. Tom is being charged."

"Cool." I looked around, and realized we'd made our way down toward the river. "Where are we going?"

"Around the sun."

I sighed. "Not the planet, dork. Us."

"To my enclave."

I had only a vague idea what an enclave was, but I wasn't about to ask and look stupid in front of him. We walked across a field and toward the water's edge. It was nearly pitch-black, and Preston took a penlight from his utility belt and guided us through the trees and weeds. I tripped over a root. "So, what do you have in your belt? I've seen the Taser, pepper spray, and cuffs, but what else?"

He led us around a rock outcrop. "A ziplock bag full of dried fruit."

"For what?"

He ducked under a tree branch, then straightened, shining the little light in my face. "I throw it at perpetrators, perfectly targeting their eyeballs and blinding them with fruit pellets."

I stared through the light. "So, in other words, you eat it."

"Are you done yet?"

"Whatever. I was just interested."

He opened his bag, taking out his mask and putting it on. Then he took his hoodie and pants off. The silver lightning bolts on his costume gleamed in the beam of the penlight. Then he took out another mask, giving it to me. "We need to remain anonymous."

I looked at it for a moment, then took it. It was simple, like one the Lone Ranger or the Boy Wonder would wear, and I put it on. "All right, chief. Lead the way."

He did, and a little farther on, the dark shape of a small, abandoned barn came into view. Preston turned and walked toward it. Half the roof had caved in, and the walls sagged. Preston went inside, and I followed. He went over to a rickety card table set in the center.

Once again opening his bag, he took out a small battery-operated lantern. Before he switched it on, he looked at me, his eyes glistening and wide behind his mask. "We are not *aloooone*," he whispered in a melodramatic voice. Then he switched the lantern on.

I just about jumped out of my skin. A figure stood against one side of the wall. Clad head to toe in a dark green suit slashed with gold, complete with a shiny green, full-face motorcycle helmet, it stepped forward. "Wha—" I began, then noticed other movement. All around me, figures were stepping forward, coming from the shadows. Eight in total.

They had different costumes. All different colors, some emblazoned with symbols. One of them had a patch with a red hammer on his chest. Underneath, it said "Red Hammer." Another was dressed eerily like a tiger. Another looked like a mortician with a mask on. "Death Itself" was scrolled across the forehead of the mask. I didn't know if I should run for my life or laugh at the most ridiculous scene I'd ever witnessed.

Preston crossed his arms over his chest. "I've brought the visitor."

Red Hammer guy spoke. "Okay. Can we stop with the whole dramatic entrance thing? I know it's good for effect, but aren't we above that?"

All at once, the rest of the group came forward, loosening up, saying hello, patting one another on the back.

I spoke low, directly into Preston's ear. "When you said you weren't as lonely as I thought . . ."

"And you thought I was the only freak."

"Hey, I'm wearing a mask, aren't I?"

"Yes. And you look dumb in it."

"So, what is this?" I asked, watching as the various heroes visited. I heard snatches of conversations. Stories about fighting crime, advice about where the action was, and crime rate statistics. If anything, these guys knew crime rates, patterns, and numbers better than the best cop in the universe.

Preston answered me. "It's just a gathering. When I moved here, I began trolling the Internet, interested if there was anything like this in Spokane. I'd heard about it in other cities, and I wanted to know. This is the culmination of my research."

"So, what do you do?"

He frowned. "What do *you* do when you and your teammates dress in *your* costumes and meet in the locker room?"

"Talk, I guess. Get ready for the game."

"Same here. Just don't use my name. It's agreed that we all stay anonymous."

"What do they call you if you don't have a name?"

His luminescent eyes met mine. "Nameless."

His no-name name struck me, and it made sense in a way. "So why did you bring me here?"

"I just thought that maybe you . . . ," he said, then paused. "I just wanted you to . . . I'm not that weird, you know?"

I smiled. "Dude, you *are* that weird, but not because of this. And thanks. Come on, let's meet your friends."

"They're not necessarily friends but associates. I would consider it more like—"

I cut him off, holding my hand up to his face. "Stop. Now. Okay? We're not in normal zone, but just give it a break," I said, then turned to a pudgy guy dressed like a homeless Superman and shook his gloved hand.

46

Coach Larson took his baseball cap off, scratching his head as he glowered at me. "What does that have to do with this team, Patterson?"

I sighed, glancing at the clock in his office. I was supposed to be picking up Preston for a tutoring session at my house in five minutes, and I'd thought this meeting would go smoothly. I'd figured Coach would be excited. He obviously wasn't. "Uh, sir, I was just letting you know."

He nodded dramatically. "So, what you're saying is that you want to take Jordan's place on the left side for this Friday's game because you have a scout flying up from UCLA." Not a question, a statement.

"No, that's not really what I was saying. I was just letting you know, and I thought . . ." I stopped, looking at his face. I checked myself. "Actually, sir, yes. This is very important to me, and I really think I have a shot. But I don't want to take Jordan's position if I don't deserve it."

His face loosened up. "Good, because God himself could come down and offer you an eternal position on his football team and I wouldn't change anything I do because of it. You'll be playing whatever position best suits you, and I'll be playing you the way I need to play you to win the game."

"Yessir."

He waved me off, looking down at the playbook on his desk. "Out."

I walked to the door.

"Patterson."

I turned, and he fixed me with a stare. "I'm sure that your full talents will be utilized during the game on Friday. And I'm also sure that if you play like you are able to play, you'll make the kind of impression that you'd like with the gentleman coming from California. Now get out of here."

Preston was looking at his watch when I pulled up at the school. No, not looking at it. Staring at it. I leaned over and rolled the passenger window down. "Sorry if I'm late. Had a meeting with Coach."

He looked up at me. "Do you know how long a mayfly lives?"

I turned the stereo down as he peered in the window. "No clue."

"One day," he said, getting in the car.

I drove. "So?"

"If I were a mayfly, you would have comparatively wasted seven or eight years of my life by being late."

"You're not a mayfly, and I was only twenty minutes late."

"I know, but if I were, in those twenty minutes you would have missed my birth and most of my elementary school years."

I pulled into traffic. "I called the scout from UCLA. He's coming to the game."

"So he can see your coach not play you?"

"I'm playing all right," I said, smiling.

"Most likely you'll be in the hospital because your friends are going to beat you to a pulp first."

"You're always so optimistic," I replied as he looked for something to tidy up in my car. "Something the matter?"

"You cleaned your car," he said.

I had. I'd taken every scrap of anything out, even vacuumed it. "You okay about that? I don't want to put you in a panic or something."

"I don't panic about those types of things. Just birds. Their beaks scare me."

The truth was I'd cleaned it because he was rubbing off on me. "So, how'd it go today?" I took a right on 35th Avenue.

"Fine. I think I got a question wrong on my science exam."

"I mean the shirts and stuff. You get any hassle?"

"The entire football team was wearing them, plus a few non-sports people. I was pretty happy with that, but I'd like to have seen more. By fourth period, the vice principal had made everybody either change or go home. I told him he was inhibiting my livelihood, but he wouldn't listen to me."

I smiled. "You actually told him that you had the shirts made?"

"Yes. He didn't seem impressed, but then again he's not

several hundred thousand dollars wealthier, either. I also found out who posted the first video."

"Who?"

"Your friend Mike."

I had nothing to say to that.

When we got in the house, I grabbed a bag of chips and a couple of cans of Pepsi from the fridge and took them to my room. Preston was taking stuff from his backpack when I heard my dad come from his office. He stopped at my door, peeking in. He held several printouts. "Hey, guys."

"Hey, Dad."

"Hello, Mr. Patterson."

He looked at Preston. "Brett let me know you're interested in the justice system."

Preston looked at me, then back at my dad. "No, I'm not."

My dad smiled. "Actually, you are, Preston."

Without a blink, Preston spoke. "I'm assuming Brett told you about my career as a professional superhero."

"He told me about a young man who has a strong desire to make things right in this world." He studied Preston. "Have you heard of the Spokane County Sheriff Explorer's Program?"

Preston shook his head.

My dad held the papers out. "Here. Take a look. It's a program for youth who are interested in a career in law enforcement."

Preston took the printouts, staring at them for a second. Then he looked up. "Why did you do this, Mr. Patterson?"

My dad smiled. "Not for the reasons you might think. Take them or leave them, but I thought you might be interested."

47

Lewis and Clark was the oldest high school in the city, and its gothic walls were set in the downtown hub of Spokane. Right across the street from the school were dozens of massive pillars that held the freeway up over the student parking lots. I got out of my car next to one of them. The lot was half-full at six in the evening, and people were heading across to the gymnasium for the Tigers pep rally. I wore my new jersey, and as I walked across the street, I saw Ben Lynch standing at the curb, waiting for me.

"Hey," he drawled, giving me a crooked smile. "You ready to be adored by the masses?"

I laughed. "If it's anything like Hamilton, I'll take a pass."

He shook his head. "It ain't. Most people come just to hang out, dance, and eat."

"Fine by me."

We walked in, and the band was already playing. Ben was popular, and I could see why. He had an easygoing way about him, and when he talked, he made you feel like he knew you, even if he didn't. "So," he said, "tomorrow."

"Yeah. Tomorrow," I replied as we walked up to the stage and sat with the other athletes.

"You think we can take them?"

I watched the crowd. It was different. More like a party than a church where players were worshipped. "I know we can take them. They've got a better defensive line than us, but you're better than Killinger."

He laughed. "And we've got you and Jordan."

"They're going to play dirty."

He laughed again. "Can't see the forest through the trees, Stick?"

"What?"

"Hamilton has always played dirty. Guess you never noticed it, being one of them."

I remembered Coach Williams talking one day after practice, jokingly telling a few linemen how to sneak a face-mask grab in without the ref seeing. The further away I got from it, the more I knew that Coach Williams *was* a coach I couldn't respect. "I guess you're right."

Just then, Principal Everson walked up to the microphone and officially started the rally. After fifteen minutes of announcing the players, along with applause for several accomplishments by the drama club and the debate team, he stepped down, the lights dimmed a bit, a disco ball began revolving, and the music kicked in.

With a cup of punch and several cookies in my hands, I stood on the sidelines, watching people talking and dancing. Jordan, along with his girlfriend, broke away and came over. "Hey, Stick, this is Monica. Monica, Stick. You can call him babyface if you want, though. I think it's better on him."

She laughed, holding out her hand. "Jordan has talked about you."

"My rep is already bad enough. Thanks."

Jordan flashed perfect white teeth. "It's all good," he said, then pointed to a girl standing with some friends. "Megan Forsythe. Hottie. Heard her talking about you. Somebody got an eye on somebody." He laughed, and Monica slapped his arm, telling him to shut up.

I looked at Megan, and she glanced back. She was pretty, but I wasn't in the mood to do anything much other than go home and think about the game tomorrow. "She looks nice. Hey, I'm heading out, huh?"

Jordan looked at his watch. "Seven-thirty and babyface needs to get to his crib. You got a wet diaper, too?"

"Just got the game on my mind. I want to go over the playbook again."

"You got the game on your mind; I got something else on mine," he said, leaning over and pecking Monica on the cheek. She blushed. "We'll catch you later."

After saying goodbye to some of the guys, I headed out, walking through the doors and under the streetlights. At the curb, I looked into the shadows under the bridge. I wasn't stupid. If there was a time and place that I'd be ripe for the taking, it would be here. Killinger knew I'd be at the rally.

I almost turned to go back in, then made my decision. Stepping from the curb, I took my keys from my pocket and trotted across the street. I hopped the low brick wall lining the lot and beelined it for my car, looking left and right.

As I walked closer, my chest tightened, and I was tempted to run. Unless they tracked me down tomorrow before the game, in broad daylight, this had to be the time they'd come after me. I clenched my teeth, speeding up.

Reaching my car, I unlocked it, then noticed. My front left tire was flat. Looking back, I saw the rear left tire was flat, too. Slashed. "Shit."

"You are an idiot."

It wasn't the voice I was expecting. I opened my eyes, and there, next to the pillar, stood Preston. In full costume, complete with lightning-strike tights, boots, chest plate, cape, utility belt, and mask. I gaped at him, then glanced around. "What are you doing here?"

"This is the most opportune time to find you alone. They might be stupid, but not that stupid."

I stepped toward him. "Yeah, no shit. You've got to leave, Preston. Now."

He looked over my shoulder. "Too late."

I turned toward the rear of the parking lot as figures materialized out of the darkness. As they neared, I saw Killinger, Tilly, Nathan Thompson, Perry Hogsett, Jeff Lions, and last but not least, Mike. I faced them, waiting, and Preston stepped up beside me. I whispered, "Get out of here, Preston. Now."

Preston actually laughed as he squared his shoulders and stuck his thumbs in his utility belt. "My superpowers will protect us. Just stay within my protective shield and you won't be harmed."

I tried to steady my breathing, but it felt like somebody was beating my lungs with a pipe—which in the next few minutes probably wouldn't be far from the truth. "Fuck, Preston, I'm serious. They're serious."

"So am I."

Six guys who wanted to beat me to a pulp stopped in front of us. Lance studied Preston. "Holy shit. Are you joking, kid? A superhero?"

Preston held up his hand to them, and his cape waved slightly in the breeze. "Leave the area immediately."

Lance and the guys laughed. "Ooohh, I'm scared now. Are you going to freeze us with your ice beam or trap us in your web?"

I stepped forward. "This is between you and me, Lance. You gave your word."

Lance stared at me. "I can't help it if fruitloop here wants his ass kicked. Maybe you can have hospital beds next to each other."

"The deal is off if you touch him."

Lance grinned. "There was never a deal. There was only you thinking there was a deal. You're not playing in the game, man. In fact, when we're done with you, you're not playing for the rest of the season."

"And you have to bring five guys to do your job for you. How about you and me? Just us. Then we'll see who ends up in the hospital."

"I don't need to prove anything. You screwed us over, and now you pay."

I looked at Mike. "Really, Mike? This low?" I said.

He shifted on his feet, hands in his pockets, but he wouldn't answer me.

217

My chest and shoulder muscles tightened. "Okay, then. Do it."

Just as Lance took a step forward, two shapes materialized on either side of us. Then two more to the sides. Lance stopped, looking as more shapes appeared, making a ring around them. Eight in total.

I stared.

Eight superheroes.

Preston's enclave.

There was Tiger Man. Frogger. Red Hammer. Superguy. All of them. Lance looked around. "What the . . . ," he began, then laughed. "You're kidding me."

Preston leaned close and whispered, "Protective shield."

Lance regained his composure, taking in the scene. "Whatever, man. This doesn't change anything," he said.

But as I looked at Mike and Tilly, they shifted uncomfortably on their feet, glancing left and right. The rest of the guys did, too.

Preston stepped forward, holding the Taser. He pushed the trigger, and blue light, accompanied by a zapping sound, glowed in the dimness. Lance stared at it, then at Preston. "You're a joke, kid. And I promise you this: I'm going to get you. I'm going to make you wish you were never born."

"You hear that?" a whiplike voice said. "He's gonna pick on some kid like a big bully boy."

Everybody turned, and Jordan stood there. Along with just about every other Tiger on the team; their black-and-orange jerseys flashing from the streetlights. Lance froze. Jordan came forward, through the enclave of superheroes, and walked up to Preston. "Yo, man. You were right. Thanks for the heads-up," he said, then held his hand out for a slap.

Preston awkwardly tried to, failed, then shook his hand.

Jordan laughed. "You're good, man. You're good." Then he faced Lance, his smile wide. "You got something to do, boy, do it."

Lance clenched his teeth, sweat beading on his forehead. His eyes twitched. "This is between Patterson and me. You don't have anything to do with it."

I stood, amazed. Speechless.

Jordan shook his head. "Aw, come on, bully boy. If you're good with six guys against one, you gotta be even better with twenty-seven against six."

Mike was the first to speak. "I don't want any part of this. Brett, I'm sorry. This got way out of hand."

I turned to him. "It wasn't out of hand when you came here." Then I turned to Lance. "We had a deal. We settle this on the field. You win, I quit the team. We win, it's over."

Lance, looking for any way out that wouldn't completely ruin his reputation, nodded. "Yeah. That was the deal. Okay."

"No, no, no," Jordan cut in. "You got yourself a deal with this assclown, Brett, but I got my own deal." He pointed at Killinger.

Lance swallowed, and a tic twitched under his eye. "What?"

Jordan went on. "Here's *my* deal. You look sideways at Preston here, and you'll have every Tiger on your ass like nothing else. Not that he couldn't take you down anyway with that Taser and his buddies, but same difference. He helps a Tiger, that means he's a Tiger. And that means we got his back."

Lance bit his lip. "Yeah. Sure. I never had a beef with him anyway."

Jordan grinned. "Man, you're a piece of work. Now, why don't you and your buddies get out of here before we have some fun with you."

In the next minute, the Saxons faded away, tails firmly between their legs. Jordan looked at me, his face serious. "You're going to stick to that deal, aren't you?"

I nodded. "Yeah. I am."

He clapped me on the shoulder. "I guess you got that name for more than one reason, then."

A moment later, he, the Tigers, and Preston's enclave were filtering away, disappearing into the night. I looked at Preston. "I can only say that was surreal."

He just looked at me, giving me that frog smirk under his mask. "I know. But even more surreal is that you said 'surreal.'"

48

I could hear the crowd outside as I laced up. I glanced at the clock. Fifteen minutes before kickoff. My dad was in the stands, sitting next to Mr. Silvia, who had arrived earlier in the day from California. We'd met briefly after school, and he'd wished me luck.

Nervous excitement coursed through me.

As I took my helmet from the locker, Coach Larson yelled my name from the office. Hustling down the aisle, I came to the door. "Yessir?"

He motioned me in. "I heard you had some trouble last night."

"It was nothing, really."

He adjusted his cap. "You know, one of the hardest things to do when you're emotional about something is to stay focused." He pointed out toward the field. "Every player on that defense will be gunning for you, Brett. Every one of them wants to hurt you."

"Yessir."

He raised a finger to me, waggling it slowly. "You, on the other hand, are going out there to play a game. A game, Brett. A game that could give you a bright future, but still a game."

"I know."

He looked down to his playbook. "Good. Because everything you do in this life, one way or another, is a game. It's all in how you play it that makes you a good man. Keep your head clear, trust yourself, and get out of my office."

The stands were usually a little over half full for most regular-season games, but tonight, word had spread, and even the announcer was dubbing us the Saxon-Tiger rivalry. When we took the field, I looked around the stadium. We all did. There wasn't a seat open. Ben slapped my shoulder. "You can draw a crowd, can't you?" he drawled.

I gawked. "I don't think they're here to watch a football game. More like a brawl."

He laughed over the cheers, pointing up to the bleacher section. "Check it."

I looked, and smiled. Preston and the enclave had come—in costume. I strapped my helmet on. "Let's play some ball, huh?"

Ben did the same. "You got it."

We lost the coin toss and ended up with the ball first, and after the kickoff, we took the field. Jordan on the left and me on the right. Ben called Swipe 280, which would put the ball in my hands.

As we lined up, I saw Tilly glaring at me. I ignored him. What I couldn't ignore was Mike, who was guarding me.

Ben called the snap, and I bolted. Just as I reached Mike,

intent on getting free of him, he grabbed my face mask with both hands and yanked hard, driving me headfirst into the turf. Penalty flags flew and the crowd booed and cheered at the same time. Ben swung wide, scrambling for an opening, but was swallowed by Tilly and two other guys. The Hamilton side went wild.

I was still on the ground when the whistle blew. I rose, and Mike stared at me. I dug grass and dirt from my face mask, finally understanding. Mike might hate me, but he didn't play that way. "Coach have a little talk with you before the game, Mike?"

"Doing what I have to do, Brett. Just like you."

From there on out, Mike played the dirtiest game I'd ever seen. The entire team did, but not so blatantly as the first play. That first face mask was meant to send a message. A personal one, directly from Coach Williams.

And so it went. The Saxon line talked constant trash, pulling every dirty trick they knew if they thought they could get away with it, and Tilly was the leader of it all as we pounded our way down the field. With every huddle, Ben reminded us to play the game, not the opponent, but it wore thin. Even as we fought on, we were getting hammered. Tilly was punishing our line, and I'd never seen him so focused on not just playing hard, but hurting people.

With no score on either side and halftime two minutes away, we were third and goal. Kody Morse and Jason Ward, who'd been taking the brunt from Tilly, finally had enough. On the snap, Kody backed up, letting Tilly in, while Jason came around his side. Jason clipped Tilly low and hard from behind while Kody suddenly charged, hitting him high.

Tilly found himself somersaulting backwards in midair

when another lineman launched into him, slamming him unmercifully to the ground. Flags flew even as I scrambled around Mike and Ben threw. I caught the ball, completely open in the end zone.

Just as the whistle blew and the play ended, Jason hurled himself at Tilly, who was moaning on the ground. I heard the crunch of his shoulder pads slamming into Tilly's rib cage from fifteen yards away, and even I winced.

In the next second, both benches cleared, and it was on. It took me a second to realize that yeah, it was on, but it was mostly on me. Half the Saxons charged directly at me, with Killinger sprinting in the lead.

I had a split second to decide. Every fiber in my being screamed to fight him. To play as dirty as him. To pay him back. I knew I could, too. I could pound him into the ground, and I'd enjoy every bit of it.

I squared myself as he barreled toward me, and guys were going at it all across the field, hitting, tackling, wrestling. Whistles shrieked, and coaches yelled. Just as Lance reached me, I ducked and drove to the side. He flew by, and the next thing I knew, I was swallowed by red-and-white jerseys.

It took ten minutes to sort out the casualties, and the penalties. Tilly was taken from the field on a stretcher, no doubt with broken ribs. I was full of bruises, but then again, so were most of us. Coach Larson was a screaming hurricane of rage. He benched Jason and Kody, promising they wouldn't see another play for the rest of the game, if not the season. He'd also benched three other players who had received unsportsmanlike conduct penalties.

Coach Williams stood on the sidelines the whole time. Silent, and with his arms crossed.

We were fourth and long. Coach called for a field goal. With five of our best guys benched, he summoned me, Jordan, and three other defensive linemen in for the play. I'd never taken the field for a field goal.

As we lined up, our kicker called the play. I blinked, surprised. With the snap, the holder got the ball, but suddenly he rose, just as I dodged past my man and pivoted. The holder threw the ball, and it hit me square, just like the playbook called for.

Caught off-guard, the defensive line scrambled, but they had no chance. I scored, untouched.

At the half, we were up, 7–0.

49

Silence in the locker room. The coaches stood in a line, facing the team, with Coach Larson front and center. I expected him to flay us alive, to rant and rage, but he didn't. He cleared his throat. "We are here to win a football game." He pointed outside. "We do not have a rivalry with that team. They might see it that way, and everybody else might see it that way, but this team will not. We have an opponent to overcome, and we will. We'll play straight and hard and smart, and we'll play *our* game, not theirs. That spectacle out there could have cost us the season, gentlemen," he said, staring at Kody and Jason. "I will not have any player play for himself. If I see anything, *anything at all*, that even hints of dirty play out there, I'll bench your ass, strip your jersey, and kick you off this team. You don't even need to have a flag thrown on you. If I see it, you're out. Understood?"

As one, we yelled, "Yessir!"

He smiled. "This is the best team I've ever coached, and it's not because we win, it's because of how we play. Let's keep it that way, gentlemen. Now, let's get out there and kick ass the *right* way. We can't lose if we do."

As we took the field, Coach Larson spoke to Ben and Jordan, then waved me over. "Patterson, you're going to learn today how to use your opponents' emotions to beat them. They hate you, right? They've proved it, proved themselves, and shown what kind of ball they play."

"Yessir."

He nodded. "That means you control them, and it also means you can make them beat themselves. You know how to do that?"

I shook my head.

"The better you do, the more emotional they'll play. The more you don't react to them, the harder they'll try to get you to. What happens when you play with emotions, Patterson?"

"You lose, sir."

"That's right. You go out and play the best game of your life and you'll see them crumble." He slapped my shoulder pads. "Get out there and play."

I smiled, and I did just that. *We* did just that. Coach hammered them with me. He called the ball to me eight times out of nine plays, and I could almost feel the volcano of rage coming from Coach Williams as he bellowed from the sidelines.

Mike couldn't keep up with me, and every time I saw him on the sidelines, Coach Williams was in his face. I almost felt bad for him. By the middle of the fourth quarter, we were up 28–14, and I'd scored three of the four touchdowns. Killinger was falling apart, and so was his line. He was sacked four times, threw an interception, and fumbled the ball once.

A few moments after I saw Coach light into Mike once again, we lined up. I looked across to Mike, getting in position. "You like playing this way, Mike?" I called to him.

He had not said a word since the first play, but every time he took the field after being raked over by Coach, I could see the light leaving his eyes. He shook his head, and I could tell he was done. Finished. "No, I don't."

"Then why do you?" I said as Ben called the snap. Mike was paying attention to me, not Ben, and he missed the call, caught flat-footed as I sprinted past him. Ben threw long, and as I hit my spot, five yards from the end zone, Mike was seconds behind me. The ball fell into my hands like a present from heaven, and I glided in for a touchdown.

With that, Coach Williams lost it. He charged to Mike and ripped into him. He ignored the ref, who was trying to get him off the field. Mike stood there, head down and taking the abuse. During the onslaught, Mike looked up at me, our eyes met, and he took his helmet off. He dropped it on the grass and walked away.

Coach Williams glared after Mike. I trotted past him, ball in hand, heading for the sideline. In a fury, Coach growled at me. "You got something to say, Patterson?"

I stopped dead in my tracks, and we stood facing each other, just him and me. And looking into his eyes, I realized I didn't hate him. I wasn't even mad at him. If anything, I felt sorry for him. "No, Coach. I don't have anything to say. I'd rather show you."

Six minutes later, we walked off the field with the scoreboard reading 35–14. We'd routed them, and I knew I'd won something much more important than just a football game.

ACKNOWLEDGMENTS

I'd like to thank all the great coaches I had growing up. They taught me what the true definition of being a team player is and, more importantly, that good sportsmanship doesn't have anything to do with playing a game. It has to do with life.

ABOUT THE AUTHOR

Michael Harmon was born in Los Angeles and now lives in the Pacific Northwest. He dropped out of high school as a senior and draws on many of his own experiences in his award-winning fiction for young adults. Learn more about Michael and his books at BooksbyHarmon.com.